The
Country
Cousin

The
Country
Cousin

Betty Cavanna

William Morrow and Company   New York 1967

To Dorothy Lewis Lummis,

author of the real Country Cousin, who took me with her to New York and Paris, let me sell dresses in her shop, and encountered many of the experiences described in this story. A very dear friend, she is not the prototype of Alix, but the inspiration for this fictional character and for the book.

The
Country
Cousin

One

After the long spring drought, the rain fell straight down in silver lines on the soft new leaves and the thirsty grass. At the Radnor, Pennsylvania, church, where the marriage ceremony was to be held, the last of the guests scurried from cars to the sheltering canopy leading to the entrance. With concerned attention for their four o'clock finery, a trio of women in flowered hats picked their way carefully between the puddles forming on the covered flagstone walk.

A great day for a wedding, Mindy thought ruefully, as she shook out the long skirt of her bridesmaid's dress, scattering raindrops on the worn floor of the church vestibule. Ahead of her Margaret Perry, the maid of honor, was holding her sister's train out of harm's way, while the bride herself, spirits undampened by the cloudburst, was making a last minute adjustment to the headpiece of her veil.

Even now Annette Perry, the girl her brother was about to marry, did not seem quite real to Mindy. Annette looked tall and slim and cool, standing there waiting while the ushers unrolled a length of white cloth along the center aisle. Is her poise a camouflage? Mindy wondered. Is she trembling inwardly?

Mindy, who had only a minor role in this ceremony, was trembling outwardly. Her bouquet of white daisies positively vibrated in her gloved hands. In sudden panic she pressed her wrists tight against her stomach, trying to quiet the jouncing flowers, while automatically she obeyed Margaret's gesture directing her to move ahead of the bride.

As she stepped forward she caught the eye of Stuart Perry, the bride's father, who smiled at her encouragingly, almost as though he understood the awkwardness she felt. Then, as the first strains of the wedding march floated from the organ pipes in the balcony, he reached down and tucked Annette's arm under his.

Mindy preceded Margaret down the aisle as though she were walking through a dream. She remembered to pull in her stomach so she wouldn't look fat, and she remembered to match her pace to the rhythm of the music, but she couldn't believe that this solemn young man waiting at the altar was her brother Jack, and that from this day on when he came home for occasional visits he would bring with him a wife.

In spite of the fact that Jack was twenty-two and Mindy seventeen, the two were unusually close and always had been from childhood on. They had grown up together on the big farm in Berks County, a Pennsylvania German section of the state, where Hubbard cattle had been raised for two generations. Mindy realized that they were isolated by the acres that unrolled on every side, but until recently this hadn't seemed to matter. As a small child she had been unconsciously but completely happy, toddling in the wake of her big brother. And later she had shared, vicariously, his successive triumphs. She could recall the pride with which Jack had received a blue ribbon at the county farm show for raising prize rabbits. She could remember his calm acceptance of his election as sophomore class president and as captain of the football team. She could still hear the opening words of his salutatorian address at the high-school graduation and recall the thrill that had swept the family when he won the Chesney scholarship.

The most she herself had ever managed to achieve was a nomination for freshman class treasurer, made by a loyal friend, and she wasn't in the least surprised when a more popular girl won. By then, of course, Jack was in college, but although his absence left a hole in her life, Mindy wasn't discontented. During the snowy winter months high-school classes seemed to take up most of the day, and at the end of the half-mile walk from the bus there was the welcoming warmth of her mother's kitchen and the smile of greeting on her father's lean and weatherbeaten face.

Besides, on holidays there was Jack once more—Jack coming home from the University of Pennsylvania full of a sense of adventure and a new eagerness; Jack as a more mature student, telling the family that he wanted to go on to medical school and that he was investigating a possible scholarship; Jack describing his professor of anatomy, Stuart Perry, who had twice invited him to dinner at his house on the Main Line. And finally, Jack telling them about Annette, making her sound as remote and beautiful as the Lily Maid of Astolat, until the astonishing day when he phoned to announce that they were engaged. Annette had never seemed real, and perhaps that was why this wedding did not seem real even now.

"I, John, take thee, Annette. . . ."

The voice was Jack's, subdued a trifle, but still clear and strong, telling Mindy and his parents that he was moving out of their household to a life of his own, a life infinitely more exciting than any for which his younger sister might hope.

The feeling of panic returned as Mindy stood quiet and listened. Her face was expressionless, a smooth mask for her emotions, but her stomach churned with insecurity. The world seemed to be moving past her at a dizzying rate of speed, while she stood on the sidelines, a country girl among these assured suburbanites, a little too plump, too shy, too self-conscious to feel at home in the milieu that her brother was slipping into so easily.

". . . to have and to hold, from this day forward. . . ."

To be thinking about herself when she should be attentive to the service was dreadful, but even during the Lord's Prayer Mindy could not quell her shameful self-concern. She mumbled the familiar words with downcast eyes while she fought back tears that stung her eyelids. To weep would be the ultimate humiliation. This she must not do!

An aroused pride saved her. At the "Amen" she raised her head and managed a smile, watched Jack and Annette turn and start back down the aisle to the triumphant strains of Mendelssohn; then she fell into place behind Margaret. Outside the rain had stopped, the waiting cars were quickly filled, and with a dispatch that seemed quite miraculous Mindy found herself standing in the receiving line at the Merion Cricket Club.

Luckily, she was at the end. Margaret graciously introduced each guest, and she had no responsibility except to smile and shake hands. By now Mindy felt that her smile had become rather fixed and artificial, but people seemed to expect this greeting, so she felt she should not let her facial muscles relax.

Strange names and faces floated past her: Mrs. Tisdale, Mr. Hendron, Miss Betty Drew, Dr. and Mrs. Wilson, people hazily glimpsed and at once forgotten. Then a slender, quick-stepping young woman grasped her hand with unusual vigor and said, "I'm Alix Moore, a cousin of sorts. This is quite an occasion. I haven't seen you since you were in third grade."

Alix Moore. The name rang a faint bell in the recesses of Mindy's consciousness. Some connection of her mother's . . . a young husband killed in Vietnam . . . talk of her courage in plunging into a business of some kind. . . . The bell stopped ringing, and Mindy greeted the next in line, a tall, unprepossessing young man with spectacles and a shaggy haircut who said, "Your brother and I lived on the same floor for two years at Penn."

"Oh, yes. Dana Fraser." Mindy repeated the name she had been given, then added, unconvincingly, "I remember hearing Jack speak of you."

The young man grinned. "He must have said something pretty feeble," he murmured, and seemed to enjoy watching her blush. "Actually, I was a great influence in his choice of a vocation. I taught him to spell Hippocratic."

This sally seemed to call for only a polite laugh by

way of reply. "Are you a medical student too?" Mindy asked.

Dana Fraser shook his head. "I'm interested in Asian studies," he said matter-of-factly.

"Goodness!" Mindy gulped.

To her relief Margaret nudged her gently and said, "You must meet our great aunt, Mrs. Walsh. Aunt Sarah, this is Jack's younger sister Melinda. Don't you think they look alike?"

She and Jack did not look alike, as Mindy well knew. Jack's hair was brown, crisp, and almost curly, while hers was a limp and mousy tan. Jack was lithe and muscular, while she was inclined to be soft and plump. Jack's nose was straight and definite, hers a mere blur by comparison. She had the Hubbard eyes, which she admitted gratefully. They were wide set and clear gray, with good thick lashes and an honest directness of glance.

"My dear. How very nice to meet you. And how lovely to welcome you into the family." Mrs. Walsh's voice accented her fragility. It was husky and very sweet.

It isn't me you're welcoming, it's Jack, Mindy could have wailed, because she was swept afresh by a sense of loss, but she murmured something courteous and tried to return the pressure of the hand that held hers in a velvet clasp. Mrs. Walsh moved on as the line broke up on a signal given by the bride's mother. By now a small orchestra had started to play in the adjacent ballroom, and all the younger people were waiting eagerly for the bride and groom to start the dancing with the traditional waltz.

Mindy felt increasingly ill at ease among these chattering strangers, most of whom were the Perrys' friends. She searched the throng for her mother and father and found them at the far end of the room in animated conversation with young Mrs. Moore, who held a half-empty champagne glass in her hand as though she had forgotten it.

"It's not a very big shop," she was saying, as Mindy approached and moved into the space between her parents, "but I think it's rather special. I try to carry clothes that will appeal to young people—the Bryn Mawr College students, the girls Melinda's age who go to Shipley and Baldwin, and the young married women who have to watch their budgets but still love pretty things."

Mrs. Moore smiled at Mindy as she mentioned her name, including her in the group without making a point of doing so, and in turn Mindy found herself listening with interest as her mother asked, "How long have you been open, Alix? A year now, isn't it?"

"A little more than a year," Mrs. Moore replied. "I took all of Bill's insurance money and shut my eyes and plunged. At the time it was scary," she admitted, turning to Mr. Hubbard. "But now I know it was the right thing to do. The Country Cousin has been a life-saver."

"The Country Cousin?" Mindy murmured.

"That's the name of my shop. It seemed appropriate, because we specialize in country clothes."

"I think it's very appealing," Mrs. Hubbard said.

Rather enviously Mindy added, "It sounds like heaps of fun."

"It is fun," Mrs. Moore admitted, "but it's hard work, too. Buying clothes can be very tricky, because you can make wrong decisions. Then at the end of the season you're left with a lot of things that won't sell at any price. But I'm learning!" She turned to Mindy's father again and said proudly, "For the past eight months I've been running in the black."

"Good for you!" Mr. Hubbard said heartily. "It sounds as though you're really launched."

"I still have my fingers crossed, but I hope so!" Then Mrs. Moore added, suddenly serious, "At least, I have some focus for my life. No business can begin to fill the gap Bill left, but I had to have something challenging to occupy my time and some of my thoughts. The Country Cousin has really pulled me through." Her mood changed again and she smiled. "That's enough about me. This is Jack's day! Look, I think the bride and groom are about to dance."

The four moved toward the ballroom door in time to

see Annette pick up her train, toss it over one arm, and step into Jack's arms. They danced together with easy rapport, smiling as though they were delighted to find everyone's eyes upon them, and when Dr. Perry cut in on his daughter as custom decreed, Jack caused a wave of laughter among the wedding guests because he seemed so reluctant to release Annette's hand.

Now all the younger people began to dance, and Mindy found herself out on the floor with one of the ushers named Peter Knox, a dark, remarkably handsome boy with imperious eyebrows and the golden bloom of an early summer tan. Peter seemed aware that most girls thought him attractive, so he made no special effort to be charming, behaving correctly out of habit, but barely concealing a deep-rooted ennui.

Interest me, his attitude seemed to demand. I dare you. And far from impervious to Peter's smoldering good looks, Mindy tried. She smiled up at him in a manner intended to be beguiling, and she made several abortive attempts at conversation, but she found some of the new steps he was doing hard to follow, and wasn't surprised when he turned her over to one of the other ushers with an audible groan of relief. Obviously he was not impressed with her dancing.

Nevertheless, her eyes followed him as he spent a rather longer time on the floor with Margaret. Peter was a boy she'd like to know. He might open all sorts of doors for her, because he probably moved in a social group that she had never encountered. Don't be silly, she scolded herself. You'll probably never even see him again.

At that moment Dana Fraser appeared at Mindy's shoulder. "I've been waiting for you to be free," he said with intended gallantry, but his words fell dully on ears so recently attuned to Peter's husky drawl. He held out his arms, and Mindy slipped into them with a stifled sigh, knowing in advance that he would dance conservatively. At least, he was easy to follow, and she didn't feel compelled to make small talk.

Instead, she was completely quiet, and this didn't seem to disturb Dana at all. He marched her around the floor deliberately, asking after a while, "Where do you go to school?"

"I'm between high school and college," Mindy replied.

Dana raised his eyebrows and held her off speculatively. "Aren't you rather young?"

"A little," Mindy replied. "Our school got overcrowded, so a group of us skipped sixth grade."

"Nice work if you can do it. What college?" Dana persisted.

Reluctant to admit that she had been turned down by her first two choices, Mindy replied, "I'm not sure yet."

A feeble remark, but Dana was apparently prepared to let it go. "What are you interested in?"

"Interested in?"

"Yes. What do you want to do? Be a computer programmer, get married, or both?"

"Neither," said Mindy, "at the moment."

"Well, you can always learn Chinese."

"Is that what you're studying?"

Dana nodded. "Chinese and Sanskrit."

"Why?"

"Why not? I'll probably teach Oriental philosophy."

Mindy looked at her dancing partner more searchingly and discovered that he was probably older than she had assumed. "Are you out of college?" she asked.

"Just. I'm going to the Sorbonne this fall."

Confused, Mindy frowned. "But I thought you said Chinese, not French."

"I'll be working with French professors, but *studying* Chinese."

"You mean you speak French too?"

Dana nodded offhandedly. "I lived abroad for a year and went to a French school."

It was all a little beyond Mindy, so she began to lose interest. She caught a glimpse of Peter's brooding face over Dana's shoulder and decided her partner was entirely too bookish to be worth much effort. Moreover, he looked rumpled and a little unkempt among these smooth, well-dressed people. She wondered what Jack and he had found in common to lead them to become friends.

But she wasn't curious enough to pursue the subject, and when the music stopped she parted from Dana politely. Finding herself without a partner, she crossed the room to rejoin her parents, who were again talking to Alix Moore. Out of the corner of her eye she could see Annette and Jack, hand in hand, approaching a round table where a wedding cake rose in tiers of fluted white icing, but she didn't follow. Somehow she didn't want to watch the cake cutting, even though Margaret called to her. "I'll be right there," she promised, and turned away.

Mrs. Moore seemed to understand her impulsive retreat. As the Hubbards walked over to watch the ceremony, she said, softly, "I suppose you're feeling a little cut off. It's only natural."

Mindy stared down at her satin slippers, now rain-stained and rather soiled. She didn't want sympathy. She didn't even want understanding. Yet she found herself admitting, "It's going to be a lot different. I mean, we live so far out and all. Mother and Daddy get along fine without people. They have each other." Then she looked up and asked, almost compulsively, "But what am I going to do all summer?" The months seemed to stretch endlessly ahead.

"I know what I'd do," said Mrs. Moore. "I'd read all the books I'm always wanting to get to." Then, noting Mindy's instinctive retreat, she apologized. "I'm sorry. I was forgetting how young you are. It must get lonely, out there on the farm."

Mindy nodded, not trusting herself to speak.

"Why don't you get a job?" her cousin asked suddenly.

"Where?"

"A fair question. I suppose you have no car?"

Mindy shook her head.

Mrs. Moore seemed to be thinking. She stepped back a pace and looked Mindy up and down, as though she were considering. "How old are you?" she finally asked.

"Seventeen," Mindy replied unenthusiastically.

"Hm."

"And I haven't any skills. I mean I can't type or anything."

"My goodness, you do feel sorry for yourself, don't you?"

This comment made Mindy raise her head and force a smile. "I'm being a bore," she said. "Forgive me. Actually, once I get back home, I'll be just fine."

"I wonder," said Mrs. Moore slowly. "I have a feeling that what you need right now is a change of pace. A little more brushing up against people. Strangers. A chance to get a sense of perspective before you go on to—" She spread her hands.

Suddenly Mindy was listening, listening intently. She felt that she was standing on the brink of adventure, and she waited breathlessly.

"How would you like to work at The Country Cousin for three months?" Mrs. Moore asked matter-of-factly. "You wouldn't earn very much, but you'd be learning something about the dress business, and you'd have a look at a different sort of life."

Mindy's eyes widened with eagerness. "You—you really mean it?" she stammered. "But where would I live?"

"With me," Mrs. Moore said. "I have a little house with an extra bedroom and bath, a couple of miles from here in Saint Davids. I wouldn't treat you like a guest, though. You'd have to help with the cooking and gardening. In other words, we'd share the work."

This was no time to tell her cousin that she was so inept in the kitchen she could barely scramble an egg. Instead, she took a long breath and said, "It sounds absolutely, completely terrific. But do you think I'd be enough help to pay for my board?"

Mrs. Moore chuckled. "I'd see to that!"

"I'd try. I'd really try!" Mindy's head swam with excitement. "Could we talk to Mother and Daddy, perhaps?"

The Hubbards were a trifle reluctant to give their permission. "I hesitate only because it's hard to give up both my children at once," said Mindy's mother.

"Promise me you'll come for a long weekend in July or August?"

Mindy would have promised anything, and Mrs. Moore seemed to feel that this condition wasn't a difficult one to meet. "When would you like to start?" she asked her young cousin.

"Any time. As soon as possible!"

Mrs. Moore smiled. "Then you'd better not go home at all. You have your weekend case, and your mother can send along the rest of your summer clothes, if she's willing to pack them up."

"Oh, Mummy, will you?" The question was rhetorical. Mindy already knew the answer. The magic carpet was woven and waiting. All she must do was step aboard without tripping over the fringe.

Two

"Nothing ever happens to me!" This complaint was one Mindy had made all too often. As she lay in a tub of hot water in the small bathroom that was to be hers for the next three months she made herself a promise never to say it again.

The hour was early, barely seven o'clock, but she had been too excited to sleep, because this day would be her first at The Country Cousin. Luckily, her room under the eaves was at the back of the house, far enough away from Alix so that she need not fear disturbing her. While trying to soak away the apprehension that was mixed with her feeling of adventure, Mindy relaxed and stared at the yellow-striped wallpaper and Swiss organdy curtains. She felt astonishingly wide-awake and eager, so full of enthusiasm that she could scarcely wait for the morning to begin.

There was no question of what to wear for this first

day of work. All she had with her that was suitable was the three-year-old green linen in which she had traveled from Berks County to Strafford, where the Perrys lived. She had pressed the dress yesterday, setting up the ironing board by the sunny kitchen window, where she could watch Alix move with her quick, light step along the rose bed, cutting an early bloom here and snipping off a dead stalk there.

Alix, as Mindy could see even on brief acquaintance, was an organized sort of person. Her house was operated on an easy routine, inconspicuous to a casual guest and far from inflexible, but a routine nevertheless. "It's easier to work within a framework," she had explained to Mindy, when she outlined her manner of living. "With the store open six days a week life is so busy it could become very hectic, and I loathe pressure. There are always times when you can't escape it, but by and large I manage to keep pretty regular hours."

The regular hour for breakfast was eight o'clock, and Alix said she usually reached the shop about nine fifteen, just in advance of the opening time of nine thirty. This schedule seemed astonishingly leisurely to Mindy, who was used to the early awakening of the farm, where the familiar noises of lowing cattle and crowing roosters usually began at dawn. Here only birdsong drifted through the screened windows that opened on her neat white-painted room.

The bath water grew cool, and Mindy climbed out

of the tub and dried herself briskly, wishing that she could towel away some of the extra flesh on her waist and thighs. Already Alix had acknowledged her young cousin's weight problem. "You'd better cut out bread and potatoes for a few weeks," she suggested. "Then maybe you can slim down from a size twelve to a size ten."

"It's hard to stay thin," Mindy admitted, "especially at the farm, where we have our own cream and butter."

"Cream!" Alix cried. "What does it look like? I haven't seen it in years."

There was no cream for the coffee on this Monday morning, and while Mindy wrinkled her nose in distaste she managed to drink it black. Because she wanted to make a good impression, she also managed to make do with only one piece of toast, although her stomach grumbled. It was not used to being treated to such scanty fare.

Alix had her mind on other things than breakfast. She was making notes on a pad of paper as she sipped her second cup of coffee; then she hurried off to make some telephone calls while Mindy put the silver and china in the dishwasher. From the kitchen she dashed upstairs to make her bed and put on lipstick, finishing just as her cousin's voice called from below, "Ready dear?"

The June morning was mild and sunny, and the drive

from Saint Davids to Bryn Mawr took barely ten minutes. Along Lancaster Avenue some of the stores, such as pharmacies, barber shops, and supermarkets, were already open, but the general air was that of a street sleepily arousing to a new week.

Mindy's first glimpse of The Country Cousin came as they passed in the car, before swinging around to the parking lot in the rear. It occupied the ground floor of a narrow, half-timbered building. Across the front there was an angled small-paned window surrounded inside by a starched ruffle framing a summer dress on a headless model. This morning the frock was lilac-colored, and below it a garden basket filled with real lilacs accentuated the color and made it seem especially desirable.

"They're dying," said Alix the minute she entered the shop, "and I forgot to bring fresh flowers from home. While you look around, Mindy, I'll phone Paula and ask her to cut a few sprays in her garden."

Paula, Mindy gathered, was habitually late, so that Alix wasn't surprised to find her still at home. "Yes, it *is* almost nine thirty," Mrs. Moore said with a stifled chuckle, "but take time to cut the flowers. We have a new helper here today."

She turned away from the phone and spoke to Mindy, who was standing in the middle of the shop turning counterclockwise slowly and drinking in the sight of all the bright and beautiful things on display. "While we're working, Mindy, it would be a good idea to call me Mrs. Moore. All the other girls do, and to use my first name might rather set you apart."

Mindy understood. "Of course. Teacher's pet is never very popular." Then she clasped her hands. "Oh, Alix, I think this is simply darling. It looks like a big doll's house just stuffed with goodies!" She ran a hand appraisingly over a soft woolen sweater, then touched the smooth leather of a bag. But the racks of bright-hued dresses were what really captivated her. In orderly ranks they marched down one entire side of the shop, then turned the corner and continued across the back. Impulsively, she walked over and inspected some of those in her size.

This behavior amused her cousin. "I always say that every girl likes clothes and boys, sometimes in that order, but often in reverse. Which is it with you, Mindy, or aren't you sure?"

Mindy flushed, as she always did when teased. "Right now I'll settle for clothes," she replied honestly. "If I owned a dress shop like this I'd never make any money. There would be too many things I'd want for myself."

"You get over it," Alix consoled her. "At first a pretty dress seems irresistible, but after you've seen it on half a dozen customers it begins to lose its charm."

"Always?"

"Well, not always," Alix admitted. "There's one girl who works here who spends half the money she earns on our clothes, because she can buy them at cost and she won't struggle against temptation."

"You mean all your sales clerks can buy dresses wholesale?"

Her cousin nodded.

Me too? Mindy wanted to ask, but she was afraid she would sound grabby.

"You too," Alix answered her unspoken question, "but not until you've been here for a month."

To Mindy a month seemed a long time to wait, but she suspected that the stipulation was a wise one. By then her taste might take a new direction. She might become more sophisticated, less of a country girl.

"That would be July—" Trying to calculate, she hesitated, then left the sentence unfinished as the door burst open and a tall, slender, dark-haired girl tugged at the key, which had stuck in the lock. "Good morning, Mrs. Moore," she called cheerfully, then became aware of Mindy, whom she obviously took for a customer.

Alix quickly cleared up the misunderstanding. "Good morning, Irene. This is my young cousin Melinda Hubbard. Mindy's going to stay with me and work here this summer, so that vacations won't leave us shorthanded."

Irene looked surprised, but not displeased. She crossed

the room and shook hands with Mindy warmly, murmuring, "How nice." Feeling shy and a trifle awkward, Mindy returned the smile and abandoned her inspection of the racks, giving all her attention to the newcomer. Irene looked poised and chic in her simple blue dress and her matching sandals. Her bare legs were already deeply tanned, and her hair was caught back in a simple fashion that was nevertheless indubitably correct. Even the purse she carried to the back room, where packages were wrapped and bookkeeping done, seemed chosen to complete her costume. Was this the girl, Mindy wondered, who spent half her salary on Country Cousin clothes?

At this moment Paula—she must be Paula because she was carrying a sheaf of fragrant lilacs—came through the back door. She was disheveled and a trifle breathless. "Here you are!" she cried, as soon as she had greeted Alix. "All the best blossoms were high up, and I got hopelessly tangled in the branches trying to reach them. Are they the right color, do you think?"

"They're perfect," Alix replied, and introduced Mindy to her. She was a young woman of perhaps thirty, who was wearing a plain gold wedding ring on one hand and a diamond surrounded by pearls on the other. Mrs. Walter Barry was her name.

"But please call me Paula," suggested Mrs. Barry promptly. She was a diminutive golden blonde with enormous gray eyes and such dark lashes that Mindy wondered fleetingly whether they were real. "How are you at arranging flowers?" Paula asked at once. "Mrs. Moore always gets me to do it, and I'm terrible."

Mindy accepted the lilac branches offered to her. "I'll try," she said, glad to have something to do. Actually she liked to play with flowers. Her mother always deferred to her on this score; she claimed Mindy had a knack.

In any event, she knew enough to pound the stems and thrust the lilacs into a deep container filled with water until they had soaked up enough moisture to keep them alive in the shallow bowl the window basket contained. While she was occupied with this chore, Paula was opening a big box of dresses that had arrived by mail, and Irene busied herself rearranging sweaters and blouses on the shelves in the front of the store.

"We call this straightening stock," Irene explained, as Mindy came to get the basket of dying flowers. "Mrs. Moore likes everything to look neat and orderly at the beginning of each day. Come over here, and I'll show you something else you'll need to know. Dresses are always hung by sizes, facing toward the right, and in each size the daytime dresses come first, then the cocktail and evening things. In other words, you work from the simpler to the more elaborate."

Mindy nodded. "What about suits?"

"We don't carry many suits. Separates, sometimes, and dresses with jackets, but Mrs. Moore feels that suits have to be very well tailored to be good, which puts most of them out of our price range."

"I see," said Mindy, more polite than sincere. "What do you mean by price range?" she asked.

"Well," said Irene, "our clothes usually fall somewhere between twenty-five and a hundred dollars, with very few things selling for more than seventy."

Seventy dollars seemed fantastically expensive to Mindy, who was unaccustomed to suburban or city prices, but before she could make any comment the shop door opened and a mother and daughter, whose relationship was obvious because they each had identical uptilted noses, came through. They nodded casually in Irene's direction, then turned with easy familiarity to the wall racks.

Mindy would have liked to linger, but she was hampered by her flower basket, which she now carried to the back of the shop. Here Paula was still unpacking clothes and Mrs. Moore was seated at the desk punching an adding machine. Without turning, Alix said, "When you finish the flowers, Mindy, Paula will show you how to sew in labels. That's as good a way as any to start."

For the rest of the morning, therefore, Mindy sat on a bench in the cluttered back room sewing silken strips machine-embroidered with the name of *The Country*

Cousin to the inside necklines of freshly arrived dresses. Meanwhile, she was alert to the activity that swirled around her. Customers came and went. Some bought, some went away empty-handed. Alix worked at her desk, while Paula and Irene stayed in the front, helping shoppers who needed assistance and letting the "lookers" browse to their hearts' content. Occasionally one of the salesgirls came to the wrapping desk to package a skirt, a sweater, a blouse, or a dress in a primrose yellow bag or box, and Mindy watched enviously. Just to handle the pretty things people bought would be a joy. She could scarcely wait until she too would be allowed to wait on customers.

Yet at the same time she felt timid. The voices that drifted back from the fitting rooms through the connecting passageway seemed disconcertingly assured, the accent entirely different from the flat Pennsylvania German that the villagers in Berks County used. She didn't want to imitate these Main Line girls, but she wished she sounded more like them. Even the slang they used was different, yet Mindy sensed that it was a habit of speech with which they had grown up.

At noon Alix sent out for sandwiches and coffee for herself and Mindy, while Paula and Irene in turn drifted back to nibble at hardboiled eggs and tomatoes. This lunch seemed to Mindy starvation fare, and for the first time she began to suspect that she was a compulsive overeater. She looked enviously at the girls' trim figures and found the sight of herself in the long mirrors sufficiently disturbing to warrant making a resolution. Tomorrow she too would adopt a Spartan diet.

The rest of the day passed quickly. Irene set up an ironing board in the stock room, and Mindy pressed out wrinkles in the newly arrived dresses, then arranged them on hangers and gave them to Paula, who attached tags to the armholes or sleeves with tiny gold safety pins.

These tags, Mindy discovered, contained a great deal of information. First came the style numbers, then the number of the manufacturer, and finally a group of code letters that specified the wholesale cost of the dress.

The business all seemed quite complicated to a newcomer, but Alix promised Mindy that she would catch on in only a few days. In any event, before she started writing either tags or sales slips, she would spend some time getting to know the stock and watching the manner in which the salesgirls dealt with customers.

Mindy was eager to learn, and she came to work the next morning prepared to observe every move that either Paula or Irene made. To her surprise, however, neither of these young women showed up. Instead two sisters, Jane and Beth Scott, arrived at nine fifteen in their stead.

Once more Alix made the necessary introductions. "I forgot to say that most of the girls work only two or three days a week," she explained to Mindy. "See, here's the schedule posted above my desk, but it isn't completely dependable, because sometimes they trade days among themselves."

At Mindy's astonished expression, Jane Scott burst out laughing. A big, hearty girl with a contralto voice, she looked as though she must wear a size sixteen and took little interest in her appearance. "It sounds like a casual sort of system, but it works," she said positively. "We all have a sense of freedom, but we have a sense of responsibility, too. You wait and see."

Beth, who was running the vacuum cleaner over the gray-green carpet that covered the floor of the dressing rooms as well as the shop, echoed her sister's opinion. "Mostly we're very relaxed," she told Mindy. "But a few things, like invoices and sales tickets, are terribly important. One wrong number on a ticket spells disaster, to quote Mrs. Moore."

Alix nodded. "You're so right. And about this we have a firm, unswerving policy. Always check your numbers twice."

Jane Scott chuckled. "Mrs. Moore's 'firm unswerving policy' is a byword around here." There was a hint of friendly teasing, but also a definite note of respect in Jane's voice, Mindy noticed. She was beginning to understand why the girls who worked for The Country

Cousin seemed so happy. They felt at ease with their employer, but they also felt the firm hand of authority.

The front door was unlocked precisely at nine thirty, and this morning a trio of teen-agers were already lingering outside the window, waiting to come in and look at bathing suits and Bermuda shorts. They chattered together like parakeets and gathered up armfuls of stock to take back to the dressing rooms, then left half an hour later without having settled on a thing.

Gathering up the scattered clothing in their wake, Mindy frowned in distress. "Doesn't it make you mad when people make such a mess of things, and then don't buy?" she asked Jane, who was helping.

The older girl shook her head. "Not really. Girls that age often want to shop around."

Actually, one of the girls did come back that afternoon and bought two pairs of shorts. She was the prettiest of the group, an ash-blonde with bangs and straight, swinging hair. She was wearing a tennis dress now and swung a racket in its wooden press from one hand, but her companion made Mindy catch her breath. She recognized Peter Knox, the dark, handsome boy who had ushered at her brother's wedding.

"Hi," he said casually, when he caught sight of her. Then he appeared to be searching for a clue to her identity. Suddenly he snapped his fingers. "Got it. Jack Hubbard's kid sister. What are you doing here?"

Three

Kid sister. The diminutive rankled, although Mindy tried to tell herself that Peter was only teasing. She couldn't bear to admit the rebuff that at first he had been unable to place her at all.

While Beth wrote out the charge slip and put the shorts in a bag between layers of tissue paper, Mindy was left chatting with Peter, who turned frankly curious. "You mean you're *working* here? That is a switch. I keep thinking of you as the Country Mouse."

Mindy gritted her teeth, but kept her smile affable. She was ashamed of liking this insolent young man, yet he was undeniably provocative. She wished she could trade places with the blond girl and walk out of the store at his side.

When the shop was empty again, Beth whistled in amusement. "So our sultry Adonis has you too in his spell?"

"You mean you know him?"

"Everybody knows him, dear. The Knoxes are right up there with the Biddles, Cadwaladers, etcetera."

This remark was too Philadelphian to have much meaning for Mindy, but she gathered that the family was socially prominent. "Peter was one of my brother's ushers," she said faintly. "I thought he was—well, attractive—but he treats me as though I were barely out of kindergarten."

Beth laughed. "Pay no attention. That's his line. He fancies he's the ultimate answer, but believe me, there are girls who have survived."

The arrival of several customers put an end to the conversation, but Mindy reflected on Beth's remark that evening while she wound her freshly washed hair in rollers and prepared to write her first letter home. Even if a survival course was indicated, as Beth had suggested, she'd be willing to run the risk of being subjected to Peter's attentions. However, she scolded herself for wishful thinking and put Jack's friend sternly out of her mind.

On Wednesday morning, upon her arrival at The Country Cousin, Mindy discovered that her name had been added to a list labeled *Stock* thumbtacked over the wrapping counter. "Mindy, ten thirty-six," she read aloud, then turned to Alix. "What does that mean?"

"It means you'll be responsible for straightening stock

in those size ranges, ten and thirty-six. That includes dresses, sweaters, shirts, slacks, in fact almost everything. It's something the girls do when there aren't any customers."

Mindy nodded happily. She liked being given responsibility. Maybe this meant that soon she'd be allowed to sell.

The day was cloudy, spotted with thundershowers, yet business during the morning became especially brisk. "In spring and summer people tend to shop in the rain," Alix told her. "You discover after a while that there's a sort of rhythm to each week. The slow times are Monday mornings, and the peak times are Friday afternoons and Saturdays. Holidays are important too. Just before Mother's Day we sell an especially large number of robes and sweaters, and before the Fourth of July we usually have a run on bathing suits and playclothes."

Like most of the details concerning The Country Cousin, this interested Mindy. She wanted to learn all she could concerning this fascinating business, and the more she discovered about the way the shop was run the more eager she became.

That very afternoon Alix took time to show her how to fill out a sales slip with the date, a description of the merchandise, and the name and address of the purchaser. Mindy learned that the original slip must always be put on a spindle along with the others made out on a given day, and that the duplicate should be handed to the customer.

Then there was the matter of paid sales, charges, and a rather complicated layaway plan, which meant holding a partly charged, partly paid item in the back room for a customer who was gradually accumulating enough money to take the purchase home. This system, Mindy suspected, was one used mainly by schoolgirls on allowances. She couldn't imagine that many of the smartly dressed young housewives and businesswomen who came into the shop would be forced to resort to such a scheme.

After Mindy had filled out a practice slip and showed that she understood the system, Alix nodded approvingly. "One more thing. You mustn't forget that handbags and bathing suits are subject to a five percent Pennsylvania sales tax. Also, it's a state law that bathing suits are not returnable."

Until then Mindy had known these facts only from a customer's standpoint. Now she would be required to figure percentages for something other than a schoolroom exercise, and the prospect alarmed her. "I've never been very good at arithmetic," she confessed.

Alix laughed. "Neither have I, but I'm learning, and I'm sure you will too." Picking up her purse, she said, "Tell the girls I've gone to the bank. And Melinda," she called over her shoulder, "you can start selling any-time now."

At this show of confidence Mindy was delighted but apprehensive. For the better part of the day she had listened to Paula and Irene, who were again on duty, talking with potential customers. Casual yet assured, they had at their fingertips a knowledge of the merchandise Mindy still lacked. They knew which slacks were cut for full figures, which sweaters would attract older women, which dresses would please the fashion-conscious young girls. By this time Mindy knew the models she herself liked, but she didn't have Paula's unerring instinct for selecting the clothes that would appeal to various types. She could now see that Mrs. Barry's habitual lateness and untidy appearance were more than offset by her positive genius at selling. Irene was clever and able, but Paula had an easy friendliness that made people gravitate toward her.

At the moment she was talking to a plain, faded little woman who said she liked to shop here because The Country Cousin carried small sizes. "You travel a lot, don't you, Mrs. Clark?" Paula remarked. "We have some new drip-dry cottons in dark colors that are really wonderful!"

Irene, meanwhile, was hurrying back and forth from a fitting room with armfuls of evening gowns. The debutante she was helping must be a quick-change artist, Mindy decided. She hadn't seen her come in, but she could hear the girl's voice, which had rare carrying quality, raised now in admiration, and again in despair. "This is just ghastly. It makes me look like a barrel tied in the middle. Let's get it off!"

Paula disappeared into another fitting room with Mrs. Clark and several shirtwaist dresses. Mindy found herself alone in the front of the shop as two girls about her own age, wearing light raincoats over slacks and shirts, came in.

They broke off an animated conversation and regarded Mindy curiously. Then one of them asked, "Is Mrs. Barry in?"

"She's busy right now," Mindy replied. Then she added hesitantly, "May I help you?"

The girls exchanged glances, and the spokesman, a diminutive redhead, strolled over toward the racks. "Well," she said without turning, "I'm really looking for something to take to the Poconos for the weekend. Something to put on for dinner and go dancing in. You know."

The astonishing thing was that Mindy did know! She knew just the frock, a wisp of pale yellow that would make this girl's hair shine like a bright copper penny. "There's a wonderful dress here, and it's in your size— you do take a six, don't you? Wait till I find it!" Mindy pawed enthusiastically through the sixes until she came to her choice, then displayed it, beaming. "Isn't this simply darling? It looks just like you!"

The redhead's companion came over and felt the fabric, rubbing it between her thumb and forefinger appraisingly. "I don't think it looks like you at all," she said to her friend in an affected drawl. "It's much too *jeune fille.*"

This term was new to Mindy, but she could guess its meaning. "I think the color would be lovely with your hair," she argued, ignoring the criticism, but the redhead had lost interest. "Have you anything else?" she asked.

Mindy showed her the rest of the possibilities in her size, then returned to the yellow dress persistently. "You're sure you wouldn't like to try it on?"

The girl shook her head. "No, I don't think so." She spoke shortly, as though she were anxious to leave, and Mindy looked after her in disappointment, feeling let down.

She was still swinging the yellow dress from its hanger as Paula came in search of another dark cotton. "Don't look so despairing, sweetie," she advised Mindy with a companionable grin. "You can't sell something to everybody who comes into the store."

"But she'd have looked so perfect in it," Mindy murmured. "And she wouldn't even try it on. I wonder why."

*   *   *

46

"What does 'soft sell' mean?" Mindy asked Alix that night as they lingered over dinner, which they had carried out to the terrace on trays. The expression had come to her mind as she continued to puzzle over her failure of the afternoon.

Alix thought for a moment. "I don't like the term, although it's used in both advertising and merchandising. I suppose it means being relaxed in contrast to being pushy. If a clerk is relaxed, a customer usually feels relaxed too."

This was a new angle. "But shouldn't you *try* to sell things?" Mindy asked earnestly.

"It isn't wise to become anxious," Alix replied. "It's important to be sensitive to people's wants and to work in their interest. You aren't going to wear the clothes you're showing. The customer is. So let the customer decide."

Mindy pondered this admonition, because it helped to explain why the redhead had not bought the yellow dress. She promised herself to try to copy Paula's attitude toward customers, but she secretly hoped there wouldn't be many girls her own age to wait on. She suspected that with them she would be especially ill at ease.

On the following day, Thursday, Alix left early to catch the eight o'clock train to New York, where she planned to spend the day in the "market." Mindy was charged with several extra chores. She had to clean up the breakfast dishes, make the beds, and get herself to Bryn Mawr by bus. The weather had turned hot and humid, and while the clothes at The Country Cousin still looked beautiful and tempting they also looked familiar. To straighten them on their hangers, to replace a carelessly sewed-on button, or to refold a stack of sweaters was no longer quite so much fun. Inevitably, a little of the bloom had brushed off the peach.

Besides, the sudden heat brought customers to the store in droves. Everybody wanted sleeveless dresses or bathing suits, and whenever Mindy sold one of the latter there was the sales tax to figure, ten percent divided by two and added to the sales slip. Each customer seemed to be in a special hurry, and Mindy became all too aware that she was slow.

At the same time she was growing increasingly conscious of the difference between herself and the other young women who worked for Mrs. Moore. They were kind to her—kind and patient—but they were experienced in a way she couldn't hope to be for a long time to come. They were also, with the exception of Jane, very chic, wearing their simple clothes with such authority that Mindy became belatedly aware of her own shortcomings. As Alix had indicated, she was too fat. Her hair needed a good professional cut, and her legs weren't evenly tanned. As for the green linen dress she had been compelled to wear all week, Mindy was be-

48

ginning to hate it. But even when the box of clothes from home arrived she doubted that she'd feel more stylish. There was no doubt about it; the girls around here dressed differently from those in the Oley Valley. Even in four days she had learned that much!

By late afternoon the rush was over, and during the last hour time dragged. When Mindy reached home with a bag of groceries she was bone weary. She was also ready to acknowledge that while her job still seemed glamorous it was frequently very hard work.

Alix arrived home at seven thirty, anxious for a shower and too fatigued to be alert to her young cousin's concerns. For the first time Mindy felt inhibited by the difference in their ages. In spite of her neat figure and youthful appearance, Alix was in her thirties, and by contrast Mindy felt young indeed.

To her own surprise, she also felt twinges of homesickness. The sunset over the hills behind the farm was so radiant compared with this suburban version. The evenings were cool in Berks County, even though summer days might be warm. She missed the space and freedom of the country, just as she missed her parents' reliable affection. Never before had she been away from the farm for more than a week!

Yet even while her thoughts strayed homeward, Mindy scorned her own childishness. Alix had been exceptionally generous and understanding. How could she ever repay her? And what had happened to her feeling that she was the luckiest girl in the world?

Such a feeling, Mindy was to discover, could not last. Reality is never as glorious as a dream, daily living never as exciting as anticipation. This her mother had tried to explain on the evening they had parted, after Jack and Annette had whirled away in a shower of confetti and the last of the wedding cake had vanished. Now Mindy began to consider the life she would lead here more practically. She'd learn a lot about the dress business, that was certain. But she might also find herself lonely in the evenings and over weekends, unless she could manage to make some friends her own age.

This contingency had also occurred to Alix, and that very Sunday she asked half a dozen young people in for brunch. Among them was Phyllis White, whom Mindy immediately recognized as the girl who had come in to The Country Cousin with Peter Knox. Also included was a neighbor whom Mindy remembered without great enthusiasm, her brother's studious friend Dana Fraser.

Dana came late and seemed to know everybody, even Phyllis, who greeted him offhandedly and went back to discussing a recent debutante party with Alix. "The clothes were simply fabulous!" she said rapturously. "Everything from New York and so new-new. You'd have loved seeing them."

"I'm sure I would," Alix replied politely, but this sort of chatter seemed to make her uneasy, and she moved away to replenish the coffee pot and put some extra English muffins in the oven to toast.

Mindy, by contrast, was fascinated by Phyllis. Covertly she watched the way she used her eyes and the manner in which she crossed her legs whenever she perched on the edge of a chair. She listened closely to her inflection and made a mental memorandum of her slang. This girl went around with Peter Knox, and therefore her mannerisms were worth studying.

Toward the other guests, meanwhile, Mindy behaved with a becoming eagerness to please. As a consequence, a thin, athletic girl, Laura Goodwin, asked her to play tennis at the Merion Cricket Club on the following Sunday afternoon. Phyllis suggested that she phone her some night if she felt like going to the movies, and a stocky lad named Gordon Blair invited her to come swimming in his pool—anytime. Mindy thanked everyone courteously, even Gordon, but with only one person was she forced to commit herself. Dana asked her to go to a concert in Robin Hood Dell that very evening, and he expected an answer right away.

Four

Robin Hood Dell was a natural, green-fringed bowl in Fairmount Park which on summer nights was filled with the sound of music. There the Philadelphia Orchestra played for thousands of rapt listeners, while fireflies winked like miniature stars in the trees and the noise of city traffic seemed as distant as the moon.

If Alix hadn't been within earshot that morning, Mindy might have fumbled for an excuse to refuse Dana's invitation, but once at the Dell she was glad she had come. Although her wooden chair was hard, the setting and the music more than made up for any discomfort. She sat as silent and absorbed as her escort, and she was sorry when the concert ended and the time came to mingle with the throng heading back to the huge parking lot filled with cars.

Dana, this evening, was an undemanding companion. He no longer seemed interested in drawing her out, which Mindy found a relief. Instead, he was apparently unconcerned by any feeling of social duty. On the drive along the Schuylkill River he scarcely spoke at all.

Since no effort seemed to be required of her, Mindy made none. She sat relaxed against the car seat, yawning uncontrollably. When they reached Saint Davids she was relieved that Dana recognized as purely routine her invitation to come in for a coke. "I've got a summer job that starts at eight," he said. "But thanks, anyway."

"Thank you for taking me to the concert," Mindy said. "I've never heard an important orchestra before, except on television."

Dana seemed astonished. "Really? Maybe we can go to the Dell again sometime before I leave."

"Leave for where?"

"For France. Remember, I told you. I'm going to school in Paris this fall."

"Oh, yes." Mindy recalled something of the sort, but by now she was too sleepy to be interested. Without lingering over good nights, she let herself into the house and tiptoed upstairs. Her cousin, who had been to a Sunday night supper party, was already in bed.

Alix was aroused, however, by even a light step on the stair. "Melinda, you had a call from your brother. He's back from Bermuda and just learned you're staying with me, so he phoned to ask you in for dinner next Friday night. I took the liberty of saying you'd be delighted. Am I right?"

"Of course," Mindy called back, but actually her delight was mixed with an emotion she couldn't define. It wasn't quite envy, nor was it resentment. She was anxious to see the apartment near the medical school where Annette and Jack were starting housekeeping, yet at the same time she felt a reluctance to encounter her brother in this new situation. In a strange way she felt almost jealous, yet was ashamed because this reaction was absurd.

In any event, the dinner invitation gave a certain focus to Mindy's second week at The Country Cousin. Each day took a definite shape, and she began to settle down and to sort people out. At first paper dolls with names and faces, the young women who worked in the store began to emerge with distinct personalities.

Irene, who looked so suave and elegant, was actually rather harried. She lived with a mother crippled by arthritis, and she had watched her contemporaries grow up and marry while she remained single. Mindy's admiration was obviously a boon to her self-esteem, but she could not entirely conceal a growing bitterness.

The Scott girls were devoted sisters, gamboling around the shop like puppies and infecting everyone they contacted with enthusiasm. Alix valued their services because the very young customers trusted their judgment. "Nobody else," she told Melinda, "can sell to teen-agers the way they can." Yet gradually Mindy recognized that Beth, although the younger, was the more aggressive of the two and that Jane's frequent errors were covered up by her sister whenever possible.

"I don't know what Jane will do if Beth gets married to this Princeton boy she's been dating," Paula said to Mindy one afternoon. "She'll never be able to make it here alone."

"Maybe Jane will get married too," Mindy suggested.

Paula looked dubious. "It isn't likely. Jane would rather curl up with a book than go out on a date. She's unexpectedly shy when boys are around while Beth's just the opposite, utterly determined to have a big Main Line wedding with all the fixings. Showers, monogrammed towels and flat silver, half a dozen bridesmaids, and a church filled with flowers."

Mindy chuckled. "That's the kind of wedding my brother just had."

"Oh, yes, he married Annette Perry, didn't he? Well, she's a nice girl, with her feet on the ground. I'd say he was lucky. But there are dozens of others who go through the motions just to be in the swim."

Of all the girls at The Country Cousin, Paula seemed to have the fewest problems. Mindy gathered she was happily married to a young architect, that she worked not only for money but because she actually loved—just as Mindy did—the pretty things she handled. She might look disheveled and even seem distrait when she arrived, breathless, each morning, but obviously she was inwardly serene. Thus she could give a great deal of herself to each of her customers.

Paula was the one who knew, before anyone else, when an engagement was to be announced or a wedding date set. She could scent a European trip in the offing for one client and a leisurely summer on Cape Cod for another, so she made suggestions accordingly. "If the girls worked on commission," Alix told Mindy, "Paula would be way in the lead. Luckily for the others I've always paid straight salaries. I don't like the atmosphere that sales competition creates."

Such a tenet Mindy had come to expect of her cousin. Alix had sound, but highly individual, business principles, and she treated her assistants more as friends than as employees. As a result they loved her, humored her, and occasionally defended her. Because no more than the rest was Alix infallible.

That very afternoon she became involved in a predicament that the girls often teased her about later. A customer who looked, according to Paula, "as though she just escaped from the Devon Horse Show," came into the store and asked especially for Mrs. Moore.

"Darling!" she cried, when Alix emerged from the back room. "I haven't seen you for simply ages."

"It *has* been a long time!" Alix was almost equally effusive. "Did I hear you've been abroad?"

The woman shook her head. "Just spending a lot of time on the golf course. Alix, dear, find something for me to take to Maine! I'm leaving tomorrow morning, and I haven't anything warm enough."

This request was a reversal of the usual, but Alix brought out dresses with matching sweaters, a pale pink knit suit, and wool slacks with jerseys dyed to match. The customer bought more than two hundred dollars' worth of merchandise and asked to have it charged.

Mindy, who was straightening stock, was in the room while Mrs. Moore wrote up the sales slip. "Let's see now, you live—"

"Steeplechase Lane, Devon," murmured the woman, as she considered a summer handbag. "No, I can't buy another thing. I'm late for the hairdresser already. Thank you *so* much. You've been wonderful, dear!"

She had no sooner left the shop with two primrose yellow boxes under her arms than Alix turned to Mindy in distress. "I can't for the life of me remember her name."

"But I thought you were such good friends!"

Alix shook her head. "I know her, of course. We met at a dinner party last winter. And I see her around, so after all the darling's and dear's I was too embarrassed to ask her name. Now what am I going to do?"

"Well, you've got her address."

Alix nodded. "But Steeplechase Lane is a long road that winds all through the back part of Devon. Well, after work it looks as though we'd better go for a ride."

At five thirty Alix and Mindy did just that. They drove out to Devon, and then slowed down and crawled along Steeplechase Lane reading the names on every mailbox. "I'm sure," Alix promised, "that I'll recognize it when I see it," but again and again her response was negative.

Not until they were nearly at the end of the road did she cry in relief. "Sharpless! Mrs. Caleb Sharpless, of course. How could I ever forget a name like that? Well, at any rate it's taught me a lesson. I won't treat another chance acquaintance like a bosom pal."

By midweek the weather changed, and Wednesday proved to be one of those flawless June days that make everyone want to be out of doors, in their gardens, on the golf course, or on the tennis court. As a consequence, few people were shopping, so Alix decided the time had come to introduce Mindy to another phase of the business.

Under Irene's supervision she was allowed to open a box of clothes that had arrived from a New York manufacturer and get them ready to be put into circulation. This process was more intricate than Mindy had dreamed. First she had to check the style number of each dress with the invoice, then write the size and description on the same invoice and date it. Next a ticket had to be made for each dress, marking it at the prescribed retail price. Then each garment had to be checked against Mrs. Moore's order and each delivered item circled in green.

"That is if it's received in good condition," Irene explained, unaware that Mindy's head was already swimming with detail. "If merchandise arrives damaged, use a red instead of a green pencil, and then make sure a letter gets off to the manufacturer asking for an authorization sticker for its return."

"Who writes the letter?" Mindy asked.

"Sometimes Mrs. Moore. Other times one of the girls. Who, doesn't matter as long as a letter gets off. Fortunately, not many things arrive in unsalable condition. The packers are pretty careful these days, and so are the workroom supervisors."

This was a comfort. Mindy went back over Irene's original instructions concerning ticketing and annotations on the invoice, then got to work.

Work? Mindy didn't find it work to take one beautiful dress after another out of their tissue nests. The shipment had come from Anne Fogarty, one of the best known New York designers in The Country Cousin's price range, and each dress seemed more intriguing than the last. There was a red linen that Mindy felt she simply must own, even if she had to save every penny for weeks and weeks. But then she came across a white piqué that was irresistible. How could she choose between the two?

Obviously the sensible course was to try them on, since they were both in her size, so she hung them inconspicuously at the very back of the layaway rack and went on with her ticketing. Meanwhile, the activity of the shop increased as girls from some of the nearby banks and offices dropped by on their lunch hours. Irene and Paula became too busy to handle the sudden influx of customers, so Mindy abandoned her task and went out to help, returning to it only after several hours had passed.

By now it was nearly closing time and Alix was anxious to leave early, because she had a five thirty appointment for a routine checkup with a doctor in Wayne, a town farther out the Main Line. "You'd better come along with me, Mindy," she proposed. "I'll drop you off at the supermarket with a grocery list, then pick you up on the way back."

"I still haven't finished unpacking the Anne Fogartys," Mindy reminded her cousin.

"That's all right. I'll take over," Irene said helpfully. "You'd better hurry, Mrs. Moore. It's getting late."

Picking up her purse, Mindy scampered out of the shop at her cousin's heels, and by the time she returned the next morning the big packing box had disappeared and the new collection of dresses was neatly hung, by their appropriate sizes, in the racks. During a lull in the morning business, Mindy found time to try on the red linen and the white piqué, persuading Beth and Jane to help her decide between the two.

"The red has more style," Beth said promptly, "but it makes you look heavy. The white's more slimming-thinning as our younger brother used to say."

As a consequence, Mindy immediately felt she must have the red, which after all had been her first choice. "I'll take off five more pounds," she promised. "In two weeks I can certainly take off five more pounds."

"I know a good reducing exercise," Beth suggested impishly. "You sit down at a table, and you do this." She put both palms out in front of her and pushed against the air.

Mindy chuckled, then said sadly, "I wish there were something you could eat that wasn't fattening, or I wish I weren't so hungry all the time."

"Eventually your stomach shrinks," Jane said comfortingly. "Then temptation is easier to resist. But," she added with a sigh, "you can't prove it by me."

Mindy still looked dubious. She went back to the fitting room and turned once more before the long triple mirrors, imagining herself as she *could* look in the red linen dress. And since she was daydreaming about the future, she also tried to imagine wearing this dress out on a date—a date with Peter Knox. He'd have a convertible with black-leather bucket seats, and she wouldn't mind a bit if her hair blew, because in the red dress she'd look so dashing, so—what was the word Irene had used yesterday?—so *soignée*.

"Mindy!"

Awakening from her daydream with a start of guilt, Mindy unzipped the linen dress and stepped out of it carefully, hurried into the cotton knit she had been wearing and answered Jane's call from the back room. "Want to help me ticket this shipment of Villager jerseys? I'll write them and you pin them on."

By the time this job was finished lunchtime was near, and as usual the girls ate in shifts in the back room. Since midmorning Alix had been seated at her desk doing paperwork, and to Mindy she seemed especially preoccupied. "Is there anything I can do for you?" she asked timidly.

Alix shook her head. "I don't think so. Irene finished unpacking the Fogartys, didn't she?"

Mindy nodded. "Why? Is anything wrong?"

"Two dresses missing from the shipment," replied her cousin. "I've just written the manufacturer to report the error, but it seems odd. This is an especially reliable house."

Two dresses. Immediately Mindy's mind flew to the red linen and the white cotton, but they were out front in the racks, exactly where they should be. After all, hadn't she just tried them on? Alix turned back to the desk, suggesting, "I wish you'd check again, please. There should be two number 376's and two 149's in size ten. Irene reports she unpacked only one of each."

Mindy went out to the front of the shop, feeling vaguely apprehensive. The moment she checked the model number on the red linen, 149, she realized what had happened. "Oh, Alix, it's my fault!" she cried, hurrying back to her cousin's desk.

"Mrs. Moore in the shop, please," Alix reminded her. Then she asked rather brusquely, "Your fault? What do you mean?"

By now Mindy was pushing aside the clothes at the back of the layaway rack, and an instant later she pulled out the two missing dresses. "They were so darling," she explained apologetically, "and they were in my size. I put them aside until I could try them on, and then when I saw them in stock I just took for granted Irene had found them. I didn't know there were *two* in the same size, so it didn't seem at all peculiar when they—the other ones, I mean—were in the racks this morning."

Alix merely shook her head.

"I *am* sorry!" Mindy continued, feeling worse by the moment. "It was awfully stupid of me. I just didn't think—"

Alix tore up the letter she had just signed, then reached for her pocketbook and extracted a dollar from her wallet. "Please go to the drugstore and get me an egg-salad sandwich on rye and a carton of iced coffee," she suggested, not unkindly. "And from now on remember, Mindy, that our firm, unswerving policy is *never* to open a box without writing down what is in that box. I have to pay for everything the manufacturer lists on his invoice, and I want to be certain that I really receive the full shipment."

"Our firm, unswerving policy," Mindy repeated to herself like a refrain, as she hurried down the street.

Five

Riding in to Philadelphia on the train, which she caught at Bryn Mawr station after work on Friday afternoon, Mindy once more felt apprehensive, but this time for quite a different reason. As always, she was eager to see Jack, yet she couldn't predict how she'd feel about Annette in her new role. Jealousy was childish, but it was difficult to snuff out the flame that singed her now and again.

She sat very still on the green-plush seat, staring alternately at the short white cotton gloves on her hands and at the trees and houses streaming by the window. It's terribly nice of them to ask me for supper, she told herself. After all, they must still be unpacking and not in the least ready to entertain guests. But, of course, this thinking was superficial and had nothing to do with the fact that she was nervous because she felt inadequate—inadequate and very, very young.

Across the aisle there was a girl, also alone, who could not be much more than her own age, but who looked capable of coping with anything. Her expression was serene, and as she glanced up from time to time from the book she was reading Mindy was impressed by the gleam of intelligence in her calm blue eyes.

When the train pulled in to Thirtieth Street Station they both rose, and as the girl stepped into the aisle she knocked her elbow against the edge of the seat and the book fell. Automatically, as Mindy stooped to pick it up, she read the title and was surprised to find that it was not a novel but a book of critical essays about contemporary art.

"Thank you," the stranger said in a soft, well-bred voice. She smiled absently, tucked the book once more under her arm, and within a few seconds had disappeared into the throng on the station floor.

As Melinda stared after her, she felt more keenly than ever her lack of direction and self-confidence. But at the moment she was confronted with the problem of finding her way to her brother's apartment. She had the street address and a rough map, sketched on the back of a Country Cousin sales slip by Alix. "You won't need a taxi," she had advised. "It isn't a long walk."

The apartment wasn't far, actually, but the streets surrounding the university were unfamiliar and poorly marked. Mindy walked for half an hour and asked questions of three likely pedestrians before she arrived in front of a nondescript four-story row house, on the third floor of which the newlyweds must live.

The corridors, like the façade, were unprepossessing, but a hall door, flung open by Jack in response to her knock, revealed walls fresh with new paint and a roomful of furniture and packing cases that looked simultaneously disheveled and welcoming.

"Mindy?" Annette called from somewhere out of sight. "Hi! We were beginning to worry about you."

"I got lost," Mindy confessed, slightly breathless from her climb upstairs. She was beaming at her brother, almost foolishly glad to see him. "Was Bermuda fun?" she asked, for want of something more appropriate to say.

Annette was the one who answered. "Marvelous, simply marvelous!" she cried, coming into the room with the light, dancing step that always made Mindy feel she was heavy and awkward by comparison.

"We had a ball," Jack said, and held his sister off by the shoulders to look her over. "Hey, you've slimmed down in two weeks!"

Mindy was so delighted with the compliment that her self-consciousness disappeared. "That's the nicest thing you could possibly say!"

Annette was equally enthusiastic. "You look terrific. And how heavenly to be working at The Country Cousin." She glanced at Jack slyly. "I'm almost envious."

"She is envious of nobody and nothing," Jack contradicted. "She just loves being a housewife. Take a look at the mess this place is in!"

"Wait until a week from today," Annette begged Mindy. "Wedding presents keep on arriving, and after all—" She spread her hands to explain and yet embrace the confusion. "Clear off that little table in the corner, will you, darling? We've got to eat somewhere. And Mindy, come on out and see my kitchen. It's only half as big as my mother's refrigerator."

This was not far from the truth. "A pilot kitchen, it's supposed to be called. So I tell Jack I'm a pilot, not a cook." She added, in a whisper, "I just bought a book on 178 ways to fix hamburger. Guess what we're having tonight!"

"Hamburger," Mindy replied with a laugh. Feeling constrained with anyone as ebullient as Annette was impossible. At the wedding Mindy had considered her dignified and remote, but this evening she seemed completely relaxed, as young and full of fun as a teen-ager. And she could tell by the way Jack and his bride teased one another that all was well between them. Resolutely Mindy quelled a needle-sharp prick of envy. Good fortune had always tagged at Jack's heels. She was happy for him—happy for both of them—but she began in that instant to have a faint glimmering of why she had these twinges of jealousy. She was too old to bask in the limelight with which Jack was repeatedly surrounded. Now it was time that she herself had a taste of success.

Mindy was unaccustomed to being self-analytical, but that night, as she rode the Paoli local back to Saint Davids, she thought constructively about her own life. She had been wasting time; that was obvious. Summer after summer she had loafed around the farm, reading romances and dreaming about an impossible future, because she was not committed to anything in the present. Now she knew she had been bored.

Bored with a lack of challenge. Bored with the empty evenings when her parents looked happily at television and she wandered restlessly from room to room. Bored with the women's magazines to which her mother subscribed and with the novels she borrowed from the local library. For how many years had she been marking time in Jack's shadow? She dared not count.

The time past had escaped her; she had frittered it away, and it was unrecapturable. The time ahead, however, was hers, all hers! And in this brief fortnight with Alix Moore she had seen, as through a window flung open, the myriad ways in which it could be saved or spent.

In Mindy's view from the farm college hadn't seemed important. It was a way of putting in four years, and it would be a pleasant change of environment, but the opportunity to study had appeared incidental. Tonight she realized that her cousin's education at Smith and Paula's at Swarthmore had given them reserves and interests that would last all their lives. When Alix was at home she didn't talk about clothes. She talked about the book she had just finished reading, an exhibition of Manet's paintings at the Philadelphia Art Museum, a French movie playing in Wayne, a new hybrid rose she wanted for her garden. Her tastes were catholic. "The Country Cousin is my business," she explained to Mindy. "Clothes are fun, and I love them, but these things are my life."

Her life was a good one, as full as the life of a young widow could be. When Alix spoke of her dead husband, she mentioned his name naturally, with a tenderness from which, Mindy felt, sentimentality deliberately had been drained. Alix had many friends and didn't hesitate to accept invitations that did not include her young cousin. She made no apologies, but would hurry off to a dinner party, a concert, or the summer theater, calling, "See you later, dear. Have fun!"

At first that word *fun* had rankled, but now Mindy knew that Alix cherished an evening at home alone. Never at a loss for things to do, she assumed that Mindy was equally independent.

But this was too much to expect. Mindy recognized, among her limitations, the fact that she was too young and too inexperienced to know how to fill several hours in an empty house. Tonight, however, she came to a decision: I'm going to start living my own life.

Just what this resolution implied Mindy didn't quite know, perhaps a search for identity, a quest to discover herself. What kind of person did she want to be and what kind of work did she want to do? A dozen basic questions were begging to be answered. . . .

"Saint Davids—Saint Davids!" bawled the conductor from the end of the coach, and Mindy jumped to her feet with a start. "I almost missed my station," she confessed.

"Dozed off, eh?"

"No. No, I was just thinking." This answer seemed to amuse the gray-haired old trainman.

"Thinking," he said, "can be mighty hard work."

By chance Alix echoed this opinion the next afternoon, when she was substituting at the store for Irene, who had gone home with a migraine headache. "I actually love to be out front here, selling," she said to Mindy. "It's so—so sort of sociable, in contrast to working at a desk or buying clothes in the New York market. Buying can be very tiring, because you have to think every minute of the time, and thinking is really hard work!"

A middle-aged woman led by a poodle came into the store, glanced at Mrs. Moore and said, "Just ignore me. I'm not going to buy anything. I'm looking for something in size nine for my daughter. She hasn't a thing to wear, and she couldn't care less."

Alix made a sound between a chuckle and a cluck, indicating complete understanding. "The nine's are over there on your right," she said. "Take your time, and if you have any questions we'll be here."

Half an hour later, while Mindy was waiting for another customer to decide on a summer handbag, the poodle's owner walked out with two dresses for her daughter and a negligee for herself. By this time the dog had become completely bored with shopping, and he was dragging his mistress along so fast she could scarcely keep her footing. Alix, watching her from the window, smiled. "You never can tell who is going to buy," she murmured to Mindy when they were again alone. "The girls play guessing games and tag this person a buyer and that one a looker, but you never can tell."

This element of chance was one of the things that made the business interesting, but it wasn't the only thing. Mindy had already discovered the thrill of seeing a pretty girl try on a dress that was indubitably right for her. She had agonized with a secretary who had to count her pennies, but who had found an outfit that she needed for a special occasion which might conceivably change her whole future life. Because she herself believed in the importance of clothes—look at the way

72

the red-linen dress made her feel—she was sympathetic and patient.

When a plump woman came in breathlessly just before closing time and wanted to try on bathing suits— "I simply can't struggle into my old one, and we're going to this swimming party tomorrow!"—Mindy showed her everything in her size and told her not to hurry in making a selection. Alix was at her desk figuring out the D.B., as all Country Cousin employees familiarly called the Day's Business. When Mindy came back to wrap the purchase and add one more charge slip to the lot, Alix glanced up and whispered, "Thank you for taking her off my hands. Lock the door, and we'll shut up shop. Look at that clock!"

The hands stood at five fifty, a full twenty minutes after closing time, but Mindy didn't mind. Her customer thanked her profusely and went off so happily that the effort seemed well worthwhile.

This attitude elicited a spontaneous compliment from Alix. "You've learned a lot in two weeks, Mindy."

"I've made some terrible boo-boos, too."

Alix shrugged. "We all make mistakes. Don't keep on worrying about them. I wasn't very happy over those missing dresses," she admitted frankly, "but I've forgiven you. In fact, I've forgiven you so completely I'm going to offer you a sort of bonus. How would you like to go to New York with me next week?"

"New York?" Mindy's eyes shone.

"It's a city on the eastern seaboard," Alix teased. "And there's a district called Seventh Avenue that is the heartland of American fashion. I thought you might enjoy seeing what it looks like, from the inside."

"You mean you'll take me with you on a buying trip. Oh, Alix, I'd adore it. I'll be quiet as a mouse and —and everything." With clasped hands Mindy felt so full of anticipation she was about to burst. Then her eyes suddenly clouded. "Except—"

"What?"

"Except," Mindy wailed with a concern that was completely genuine, "I haven't got a thing to wear!"

74

Six

Mindy had been to New York for the World's Fair, but the garment district was a new experience. As she and Alix emerged from the confusion of Pennsylvania Station the sidewalk heat seemed to bounce up and hit them. Already a brazen sun was blistering the crowded streets, and most of the people jamming the crossings appeared to be racing to keep appointments for which they were already late.

By contrast, Alix looked composed and cool. She was wearing a simple black-linen dress, and she had advised Mindy to settle on a sensible dark cotton. "We don't have to be chic," she said, "but we do want to be comfortable."

As at home in this Seventh Avenue milieu as she was in her Saint Davids' garden, Alix turned Mindy uptown, for her first encounter with the wide ribbon of a street unwinding toward Times Square. Bulky trucks

lined every crosstown curb, while others prowled in
search of a parking space. Delivery boys wheeled racks
of dresses, suits, and coats, some in heather tones,
browns, or blacks, others as bright as holiday balloons.
Hand trucks abounded, and as Alix sidestepped to
avoid one rocketing toward her she made a wry comment. "Somebody has called these carts the greatest
pedestrian hazard since the coaches of the French aristo-
crats stopped running down the poor in the streets of
Paris. Fortunately, we haven't far to go."

Indeed, within the next block she turned into the
door of a building known simply by the number 550
on its door. "The worst is over," she told Mindy cheerfully. "All the showrooms are air-conditioned."

At a bank of elevators a dozen women and a few
men were waiting as anxiously as though the trip to the
upper floors would be their deliverance. Alix and Mindy
joined them and, wedged like asparagus stalks in a tin
can, zoomed upward. "Here we are," said Alix suddenly, and caught Mindy's hand, pulling her between
two men who were arguing about something called
"loss leaders."

Before Mindy could ask, "What's that?" she found
herself following her cousin through a door into a bright
room hung with contemporary paintings. "Goodness,"
she breathed, "is this a showroom?"

Alix nodded. "Another manufacturer may decorate

his place like a Hawaiian *lanai*. Still another may imitate a Paris boutique. It all depends."

"Paris," echoed Mindy, and thought fleetingly, "I'd like to see Paris someday."

At the moment, however, she was busily absorbing first impressions. Every detail fascinated her: the bronze-green color of the carpet, the sight of skyscrapers through the huge windows, and the glimpse of a stock-room full of clothes as a door swung open. A young man in a dark suit appeared, his lean face lighting in recognition.

"Alix!" he cried. "How are you, dear? I'll be with you just as soon as I finish with Maude." More confidentially he added, "She's from Kansas City, and she's got a plane to catch."

Alix nodded and smiled, then headed toward a low table on which there were sharpened pencils stamped with the manufacturer's name, along with a couple of pads of order blanks, the top sheets neatly interleaved with carbon paper. "Sit down," she said to Mindy, pulling up another chair. "We'll be here for quite a while."

During the next few minutes Mindy had a chance to look around at two other buyers already occupied with salesmen, working from racks containing fifteen or twenty dresses. These items they displayed in rapid sequence. A very plain, large-boned young woman, whose straight hair was pulled back severely and fastened with a ribbon, and whose costume looked more appropriate for a walk in the country than for a day in New York, was making decisions with astonishing rapidity. She was seated within overhearing distance, and Mindy listened to the interchange.

"I've already got that one. Show me the first again."

"Let me tell you, hon, this one is tremendous. It's walking out all over town."

"Sure, at ninety degrees in the shade, a woolen as thick as a horseblanket is marching up Fifth Avenue."

The salesman grinned and held up another dress. "This checked out very nice."

The buyer nodded. "I can use that one. What's the number? Usual sizes? Delivery?" She was writing rapidly as she spoke.

The next sample shown was an elaborate short cocktail dress. "Too jazzy for me," the buyer said at once. "What do you have in black? Your little blacks are usually good."

The rest of the dialogue was lost on Mindy, because at this moment the young man who had been helping the Kansas City buyer came over. Quickly, Alix introduced her young cousin. "Mindy's learning the dress business this summer," she said.

"You've got a good teacher," replied the young man, whose name was Eddie.

"Pure flattery," Alix said to Mindy. "He knows I'm new at the game."

Meanwhile, Eddie was removing the first of a series of dresses from the rack he had wheeled over. All were daytime wools, and each sample was displayed in a single color. "Here are the other colors available," he said to Alix, and handed her a swatch card with intriguingly named shades. Tahiti, Mindy discovered, was a rich, deep blue; grenadine a singing red; and seaweed a dark moss green.

As he showed each dress—with the same speed at which the other men worked—Eddie quoted wholesale prices. But Mindy knew that in each case Alix must calculate not only the selling price, but try to decide whether her customers would be interested in the garment at thirty-five, fifty, or seventy dollars, as the case might be. She too tried to make similar estimates, but within a few minutes she found that her head was spinning in the effort to keep up.

"You have this body in a raw silk right now," Eddie said of a sample he called a "very strong dress," apparently meaning that it had been especially successful in the summer line. "Now we're doing it in a lightweight wool."

"A *body*," Alix took time to explain, "is the style of a dress, and it may be repeated in several different fabrics with minor variations. If it's really good it's often cut a second season."

By now Eddie had a nubby tweed in his hands. "This one's terrific! It's on every order."

Mindy looked enviously at the sample swinging enticingly from its hanger, but Alix shook her head. "Too high style for Philadelphia. Save that one for New York and Dallas. My customers like understated clothes."

Eddie nodded and passed two dresses that were obviously in the same category, then held up a simple gold tweed trimmed with grosgrain ribbon.

Alix nodded, but she still had done no more than fill in the address of The Country Cousin at the top of the order blank. Not until she had looked through both this rack and two others did she appear ready to make a decision, and Eddie seemed familiar with this procedure. He passed the last three dresses on the third rack, then asked, politely, "Now do you want to write?"

Mrs. Moore nodded and picked up one of the sharpened pencils. Again Eddie started through the first rack, this time passing by many of the samples in which his client had showed no interest and concentrating on the ones she had approved. Mindy watched quietly, interested in the speed and harmony with which they worked. In ten minutes the order was finished, all the style numbers, quantities, descriptions, and sizes carefully filled in, and the delivery date noted. At once Alix stood up to leave. "Thank you, Eddie," she said agreeably.

"Thank *you*," Eddie said, and walked with them to

the door. "If you want to reorder that gold tweed, Alix, better do it early. It's sure to be a Ford."

"A Ford? What does he mean by that?" Mindy asked, while she and her cousin waited for the elevator.

Alix smiled. "That's Seventh Avenue slang. A Ford is a style that sells so remarkably well that it's reordered again and again. We also call it a *runner*. Does it all sound like Greek to you?"

"It sounds like gibberish when you get to talking fast," Mindy admitted, "but I think it's enormous fun. The clothes are all so marvelous! I don't see how you ever decide."

"A buyer gets to know her own customers," Alix said, "and the things they like to wear. The salesman can be a great help. Eddie, for instance, knows my business, what I like, and which colors are proving most popular. He's a valuable source of information, but in the end the decisions must be mine."

"Doesn't spending so much money scare you to death?"

"It did at first, but now I know that everybody buys a certain number of dogs. It's like a guessing game. If I guess right ninety percent of the time I'm a winner, and if I guess right eighty-five percent of the time I'm still not a loser. After the Fourth of July we'll have a sale, and you'll see what happens to the markdowns. A lot of them will walk out in a very few days."

"Does *walk out* mean to be bought?"

Alix nodded, then laughed at herself. "This atmosphere is infectious. I'm here for an hour, and I begin to use the garment trade colloquialisms as naturally as everyone else."

"Is that wrong?" Mindy asked.

"No, but I think all slang is a bit sloppy. It implies that your vocabulary is limited."

As she spoke Alix was opening the door of another showroom and Mindy walked into a small lobby hung with fishnets and lobster buoys and carpeted with a bright rag rug. Behind swinging doors made from old shutters was a chintz-curtained room furnished with Cape Cod pine and filled with playclothes—striped jerseys, shirts, shorts, slacks, tennis dresses, and bathing suits, besides a number of ridiculous beach hats, which lay like oversized flowers on several chairs.

In spite of the inviting array there were no other buyers in the room. "I'm going to reorder some jerseys," Alix explained. "It's out of season for this house, you see. The summer line is almost finished."

Instead of the sophisticated air of the previous showroom this little place had a casual and intimate flavor. The owners were a young couple named Nickerson, who knew Alix well and who had been in business for only a few years themselves. Mindy could see that their enthusiasm about their own designs was contagious, because when Alix left she said with a sigh, "I bought too much there, but they're irresistible."

By now it was twelve o'clock. "Let's have an early lunch," Alix suggested. "I'll take you to Wilkinson's. It's a big, noisy restaurant, where all sorts of people in the garment trade lunch, and it has the advantage of being practically next door."

Once more the sidewalk heat reached up and slapped Mindy in the face, and she shuddered at the sight of an errand boy who looked half-smothered by the mink pelts he was carrying. But in a couple of minutes she was once more in an air-conditioned room. The restaurant was not yet crowded, and after dutifully ordering a jellied soup and a salad, Mindy waited with Alix at an empty table. It didn't remain empty long, however. A sharp-featured man with kindly dark eyes spotted Mrs. Moore and hurried toward them.

"Alix!" he cried with considerable ebullience. "You should come to New York on a hot day. Where have you been keeping yourself? You haven't even looked at our fall line yet."

"I'm coming right after lunch," Alix promised. "Sit down, Harvey. This is my young cousin, Melinda Hubbard. She's working in The Country Cousin this summer." As she spoke Alix pushed back a chair.

Harvey, or Mr. Weintraub, as Mindy learned to call him, sank down gratefully. "So you want a store of your own, eh?" he said to Mindy. "All the young ones do."

"I haven't quite aspired to that yet," Mindy told him. "I'm only working until school starts in the fall."

"School? College, eh? That's good. Never can get too much education. That's what I tell my son Bob."

"How is your son?" Alix asked.

"He's working this summer too, packing and shipping, but he claims he hates manufacturing. Wants to be a chemist. Can you imagine when he has a made-to-order business to inherit. I don't know what to make of him, Alix, and that's a fact."

Alix merely smiled. "Bob's a bright boy, Harvey."

"Bright, yes, but sensible, no." Harvey shrugged. "Well, you can't have all the luck." Then he changed the subject. "How's business? Selling any clothes?"

"A few, Harvey, a few."

Harvey reached out and patted Alix's hand. "Good girl," he said softly, almost tenderly. Then he turned to Mindy. "I've known her from the start," he said, "and I knew she could do it. A smart one, your cousin."

"Mr. Weintraub was the most enormous help to me," Alix told Mindy. "When I was getting started the market frightened me. Everybody seemed so sharp and sure of themselves."

Harvey winked solemnly. "That's just a front."

"Anyway, Mr. Weintraub was my first real friend on

the Avenue," Alix continued. "He's saved me from many a bad choice." Then in a lighter tone she added, "And fortunately he makes the kind of classic clothes Main Line women live in—good tweeds, nice cottons, and well-cut linens—things that are in style, in one version or another, year after year."

Harvey glanced around. "I thought Bob would be along by now, but maybe he brought a sandwich from the apartment. He claims I don't pay him a Wilkinson wage."

Such proved to be the case, because not until the three took the elevator to one of the top floors in the same building did Mindy have a chance to meet the much-discussed son. Then Mr. Weintraub suggested that Bob show her the factory. "We're one of the few remaining houses with a workshop right next to our showroom," he said proudly. "It costs money, but we like it that way, because we can keep a close eye on production." He turned to Alix. "Do you want to look at the transitional cottons first, or go straight to the fall things? I think this is the greatest line we've ever done."

This was in effect a dismissal, and Mindy found herself alone with a young man of perhaps nineteen who did not in the least resemble his father. He was nearly six feet tall, with deep-set eyes of such a dark blue they looked black, except when the sunlight caught them. He wore a light cotton jacket and a pair of rumpled slacks in contrast to the neat dark suit popular among most of the young men who worked in the showrooms. Furthermore, he spoke in a cultivated voice, with none of Mr. Weintraub's easygoing use of the vernacular, and seemed not at all averse to shepherding a young girl through the shop.

In fact, Mindy's naïveté seemed to intrigue him. He took special care to explain the procedures in the cutting room, the marking room, and the actual factory, where rows of men sat at sewing machines. Among them were only two women, which surprised Mindy. When they had moved on to the designing room, she said, "I thought dresses were always made by women."

"Not always. Most of Dad's line is tailored, and men are better tailors, by and large." He picked up a sketch from a table, and said, "This is the way a dress usually starts, with a designer's drawing, although sometimes material is draped right on a form."

Mindy took the sketch from Bob's hand and looked at it carefully. The artist was not especially skillful, but the basic lines she intended to use were emphasized by heavy brush strokes so that Mindy could imagine the effect of the completed dress.

She caught her breath in admiration, and said, spontaneously, "This is the part of the business I'd just love!"

"Designing?" Bob seemed interested and showed her

some other sketches. "This is an advance idea for cruise wear, and this is going to be a zingy little beach coat, done in an imported cotton. A little offbeat for my father, but lots of fun."

"It's darling," Mindy crooned. Then, because Bob was so unexpectedly easy to talk to, she said, "I make some of my own clothes, and I'm always improvising. My mother teases me because she thinks I should stick to patterns, but it's more fun the other way."

Bob nodded. "More creative, you mean."

"I guess so." Mindy thought about this remark for a moment. "How does a girl get started being a designer? Does it take years and years?"

"I don't know much about that end of the business," Bob admitted. "There are fashion design schools, of course, but out of the hundreds who graduate from them there must be only a handful with real flair. Some of the top French designers never went to school at all."

"How did they get started?"

"Worked their way up through the shops. There's something to be said for the apprentice system, you know. If you work in a dressmaking establishment—or in a chemistry lab, for that matter—under a really good teacher, you're bound to learn fast."

Mindy nodded. "I suppose so." She walked over and replaced the sketches on the table. "Cruise wear," she murmured, chuckling. "This is such a funny business. In June you show winter clothes, but at the same time you're looking ahead to next spring."

"That's right. The garment trade is crazy, all three billion dollars' worth."

"Are you kidding?"

Bob shook his head. "If you're interested in statistics, this is supposed to be the world's most productive tenth of a square mile." He walked to the window and glanced down at the urban beehive below. "All the oil pumped each year in Texas doesn't earn as much money as the women's wear sold here. What a racket!"

"Your father says you're not interested in going on with it," Mindy ventured.

"I'm not," Bob said immediately. "This whole district is too congested and high-strung for me. I don't have the business in my blood the way Dad has. When I get out of N.Y.U. I want to work quietly in a laboratory somewhere out of the hurly-burly. Maybe even out of New York."

Mindy looked rueful. "You've never lived on a farm. I think a big city is fascinating. It's so—alive!"

"You can have it," Bob said with a shrug. Then he asked, unexpectedly, "Are you in college?"

"I hope to be next fall."

"Where?"

Mindy frowned. "I don't know yet. Not one of the big ones. I'm afraid I'm not very bright."

"Come now!" Bob chided her. "Have you ever thought of Parsons?"

"Parsons? Where's that?"

"Right here in New York. If you're really interested in fashion design you ought to consider it. There's a girl across the hall who went there, and she's done awfully well."

Parsons. Mindy filed the name away in her mind and continued on her tour of inspection. There was no hurry, since Alix was bound to be tied up for at least an hour, and she was thoroughly enjoying her conversation with Mr. Weintraub's son. As a matter of fact, when he returned her to the showroom, she left him reluctantly.

"Thank you *very* much," she said.

"A pleasure." Bob inclined his head in a gesture that was almost a bow. "Come back again with your cousin."

"Nothing," said Mindy, and she meant each word, "would please me more."

Seven

Riding home on the train, Alix seemed tired but talkative. Suddenly relaxing, after the strain of choosing so many clothes, she chatted amiably about various facets of the dress business and told Mindy a good deal about the manufacturers they had visited.

The last house, to which they had gone after leaving Mr. Weintraub, had been the most interesting in many ways. Craely carried a line of inexpensive but well-made dresses, notable for their new look and their careful cutting and tailoring. "You can't put price tags on clothes like that," Alix said. "They could cost fifty or a hundred and fifty dollars, depending on who's wearing them."

Mindy understood. "I'm going to take all the buttons and bows off everything I own," she said. "At least, that's the way they made me feel."

"You're very perceptive," replied Alix, amused. "You know, I wore Craely dresses long before I opened

The Country Cousin. As a matter of fact, I took some to Paris with me the year Bill and I met. All the American girls working at the American Embassy adored them, and when they found out how much they cost they were green with envy. You couldn't duplicate them for twice the price in France."

"But I thought Paris had the very best fashions!"

"The best? Well, perhaps, but also the most expensive. There's very little available between designers' clothes that sell for many hundreds of dollars and the very cheapest kinds of dresses and suits on the racks at Le Printemps and the Galeries Lafayette."

Mindy had never heard of these stores. "I didn't know you'd been to Paris, Alix. You've never mentioned it."

"Haven't I? It was the year after I got out of school, before my parents died. Bill was working part-time at the embassy and taking some graduate courses at the university. He came out to Versailles one night to have dinner with my friends the Lamberts whom I was visiting. Jim Lambert was a captain in the Air Force stationed at Camp des Loges."

The trip sounded incredibly romantic, romantic but of course very sad, because Mindy knew by this time that her cousin's marriage had been all too brief. However, Alix never dwelled on the past. "I remember Virginia Lambert saying she wished I'd packed my suitcase with clothes for her. She'd been abroad three years and was just dying for something new and smart to wear, but everything she really liked in Paris was more than she could afford."

"It might be a good idea," Mindy mused.

"What might?"

"To take some Country Cousin clothes to Paris and sell them. I mean, why not?"

Alix laughed, leaning back against the seat, and turned to Mindy as though she had said something preposterous. "That would be a switch! The French would just love that!"

"You mean they'd make trouble?" Mindy asked.

"I would guess," said Alix, "that they'd make plenty of trouble. There are all sorts of international trade laws and regulations. Besides, from what I could see on my one brief visit, the French government simply thrives on red tape."

She turned and looked out the window at the muddy, meandering Raritan River winding through the city of New Brunswick, and Mindy became preoccupied with her own thoughts, the uppermost of which was that she was again hungry and that dinner was still two hours away. She glanced around the car. Nobody else looked especially hungry. The businessmen with their briefcases and the women with parcels or boxes stacked on the overhead racks seemed, almost uniformly, weary. They turned the pages of newspapers or magazines as though the heat of the day had induced a lethargy not easily dispelled by the air-conditioned train.

Princeton whizzed past, fields of green with towers and a church spire in the distance; Trenton came and went. Mindy yawned and shifted on the seat. "There was a movie," she said idly, "with wonderful pictures of Paris." She searched her mind for the title, but Alix was the one who supplied it.

"*How to Steal a Million?*"

"Yes, that's it! Is Paris really like that?"

"I think it's even more exciting. No picture can quite capture the atmosphere. It's a woman's city, Mindy. Beautiful and unexpected and full of a sense of history. It's also highly individual. There's no other museum like the Louvre, no other river like the Seine, no shopping street as glamorous—at least to me—as the Faubourg Saint Honoré—" She broke off. "I sound positively rhapsodic, don't I?"

Mindy nodded. "You make me feel shivery." She wriggled as though the sensation were pleasurable, then asked, "How long were you there?"

"About six weeks. The Lamberts had a house with plenty of room, and they kept insisting that I stay."

"Do you speak French, Alix?"

"A little. Enough to manage with in stores and hotels, but not enough to conduct an intelligent conversation. I remember a good many words from my high-school

French, but I get rattled when I try to use verbs."

"Will you ever go back, do you think?"

"To Paris? I certainly hope so. Why yes, of course I'll go back to Paris! Anything else is unthinkable!"

Her cousin spoke with such forcefulness that Mindy was amused.

Her tone of voice changing to match her mood, Alix settled back again and said, more gently, "As soon as my business becomes well established I'll take a vacation. Maybe in another year or two. . . ."

The train's arrival at North Philadelphia Station put an end to the discussion, but the next day the subject of Paris came up again. This time it was introduced by a customer, a tall, handsome woman who came into The Country Cousin with her teen-age daughter, a girl with long straight hair, beautiful brown eyes, but an unfortunate complexion.

"Why, Mrs. Paige!" cried Alix, who happened to be in the front of the store redecorating the window display. "I didn't know you were home."

"We just arrived last weekend." The woman turned to her daughter. "You remember Caroline."

"Of course!" Alix shook hands warmly, then introduced Mindy. "This is my young cousin, who is helping me this summer. You girls must be about the same age."

Caroline nodded and murmured something polite, while Alix asked Mrs. Paige, "Are you still living in Frankfurt?"

"No, we're in Paris now," Mrs. Paige replied. "My husband has joined General Motors there."

"You're *living* in Paris?" Mindy asked Caroline with unconcealed envy.

The girl nodded, but without great enthusiasm. Her interest had been captured by the clothes. She went quickly over to the wall cases and started to look through the dresses in her size, sighing in admiration. To Mindy, who followed her, she said, "We only get home once a year, so we have to stock up on everything. Oh, you don't know how good it is to see American clothes!"

Mrs. Paige echoed this sentiment. In her purse, she had a shopping list, which she took out, along with her eyeglasses, as she settled down in the one comfortable armchair. Then she said, "Have you time to help us personally, Mrs. Moore? I always trust your advice."

"Of course," Alix replied genially, although Mindy knew that she had hoped to spend the next hour at her desk. "Would you like to start with things for Caroline or clothes for yourself?"

"Let's begin with Caroline," Mrs. Paige suggested. "Then maybe your cousin could work with her while we find something for me. She needs at least three sweater-and-skirt sets for school, one party dress, and something to wear to church. She never seems to have anything to wear to church."

Matching sweaters and skirts, fortunately, were carried in all seasons, even midsummer, but finding dresses that would be useful for fall and winter was less easy. "There's this tissue wool, though," Alix said. "It's so light you could wear it right now, but it would be equally good under a winter coat. And there are some silk tweeds left from the spring collection you might try, if Mindy can find anything in your size."

Caroline had her own ideas. She didn't like the silk tweeds. "Too old," she said at once. But she was delighted with some of the new colors in the John Meyer sweaters and skirts. She chose half a dozen different combinations, which Mindy carried back to a fitting room. Caroline, who could scarcely tear herself away from each new thing that caught her eye, rather reluctantly accompanied her.

Such enthusiasm delighted Mindy, and she forgot her constraint when trying to help customers in her own age group. She regarded Caroline's image in the mirror as critically as she would have looked at herself and when asked for an opinion gave one honestly. "The blue is a wonderful color, but it doesn't do as much for you as the yellow. And the skirt with the small check looks marvelous with that sweater. It's much more slenderizing than the big plaid."

Caroline agreed and hurried out front to let her mother confirm their combined judgment. She also decided on a pullover and a plain tweed skirt in an interesting shade of pink, and some slacks with a matching jersey. The tissue wool she put on only because Mrs. Moore had suggested it, then considered it more carefully. "Why, it's awfully good, isn't it?" she asked Mindy. "I'd never have dreamed!"

In the next fitting room Mrs. Paige was trying on jacket dresses in a rayon and acetate fabric that looked like raw silk, while Alix had gone up to the storeroom over the shop to get two wool costumes she had ordered especially with Mrs. Paige in mind.

Caroline kept darting back and forth from one room to the other, exclaiming over each becoming style with contagious delight. "Get everything you really need, dear," her mother advised. "Remember, we won't be home again for another year."

Before the morning was over the Paiges' purchases had accumulated until they filled three sales slips and totaled almost four hundred dollars. "I always feel extravagant when I buy so many things at once," Mrs. Paige confessed, "but last year I regretted being overcautious. My goodness, I wish you could bring some of your clothes to Paris, Mrs. Moore. Between the embassy personnel and the American business people you'd have dozens of customers!"

"The French girls I go to school with would buy things too," put in Caroline. "They love my matching sweaters and skirts. They look so *different!*"

Different? Mindy smiled doubtfully, because they were almost a uniform among American schoolgirls.

But Caroline glanced at her, and said, "I really mean it. You don't know how hard it is to get really good materials and well-made everyday clothes in the French shops. Oh, of course, there are marvelous things in the boutiques, but they're all terribly high style and expensive, aren't they, Mummy?"

Mrs. Paige nodded. "Couturier clothes are often for very sophisticated people or for the very rich. They're certainly not for wearing around our chilly apartment in Neuilly, or for marketing, or for spending a day in the country." She looked at Mrs. Moore. "You understand."

"Of course," said Alix, and Mindy could tell that her cousin really did understand. After the Paiges had left, Alix said, with a sigh, "It would be great fun someday."

"To go to Paris again?"

"To take some clothes to Paris and sell them there. It's the only way I'll probably be able to afford to go."

With this remark the subject was once more dropped. June was over, and the first three days in July brought droves of customers into the store. Some were going away for the rest of the summer, others were planning a fortnight's vacation, and still others were simply looking forward to a weekend holiday.

Mindy scarcely had time to apply fresh lipstick. She pulled stout women into bathing suits, searched for the few size-sixteen shorts The Country Cousin carried, and sold dozens of skimmers and sleeveless shells. Everybody seemed to be going somewhere—to Martha's Vineyard, to Canada, to Cape Ann, to Ocean City, to Rehoboth Beach. Most of the young schoolteachers and college girls heading for Europe had already departed, but travel clothes were still in demand. "Something that won't muss. Something that will drip dry." Gradually the stock became depleted as the more usable and attractive outfits were sold.

"All we have left are the dogs," Irene wailed one afternoon. "If I have a customer who wears size twelve and wants anything but a sleeveless cotton, I have practically nothing to show her."

Alix seemed to feel that this situation was not bad, but good. "I'd rather go into our July sale with too few clothes than too many," she said. "Besides, our fall things will begin coming in by the middle of the month. Then we'll need every inch of space we can get."

Mindy was looking forward to the sale, because it would introduce her to still another phase of the business. By this time she was settling down and beginning to enjoy herself, outside the store as well as within it. Shyness no longer made her inarticulate. She had learned to wear her hair a new way. Five pounds had vanished from her thighs and midriff. And twice a week, at least, she was playing tennis with Laura Goodwin, who proved to be faster but more erratic than she on the court. Their play evened out, so that the two girls were sufficiently closely matched to make the game sporting. And the more weight she lost the more likely Mindy was to win two sets out of three.

The Fourth of July, falling on a Saturday as it did this year, gave all the employees of The Country Cousin a two-day weekend, which they looked forward to with either apathy or anticipation, according to their plans. The Scott sisters were going to the Poconos with their parents, Paula was planning to dig a new rosebed with the help of her husband, Irene was staying home with her mother, who had been bedridden for the past week with a particularly acute bout of her arthritis, and Mindy and her cousin were planning to drive up to the farm.

Mrs. Hubbard had phoned and invited them cordially, but rather cautiously. "Unless you have something better to do," she had said.

Alix, after perfunctorily consulting Mindy, replied, "It sounds heavenly. May we drive up Saturday morning and come home Sunday afternoon?" There was a short silence broken by Alix saying, "Oh, are they? That will be nice. I'll tell Mindy. She'll be pleased."

A moment later she hung up, and said casually, "Jack and Annette are expected for dinner Sunday, along with Peter Knox."

Eight

Peter Knox! Mindy's initial surprise dissolved into apprehension combined with a secret sense of anticipation. She couldn't picture Peter at the farm, couldn't imagine him with her mother and father. Why, when he had never come home with Jack before, did he choose to drive up this weekend? Yet the thought of seeing him filled her with nervous excitement. For once he wouldn't be surrounded by other girls.

Not that she had a chance of competing with the Main Line debutantes he generally dated. Mindy was too realistic to build air castles in which Peter was the prince and she was the lady fair. She didn't expect miracles to happen, but she did look forward to meeting him again, even in such an unlikely environment as the farm.

Alix and she drove up very early Saturday morning, before the highways became crowded with holiday traffic. The Oley Valley unrolled like a Grant Wood painting, climbing in smooth rounded hillocks to the low green mountains beyond. In the fenced fields cattle grazed, heads down, all facing the same direction, and on a knoll half a mile away the farmhouse stood, its gray-green walls of serpentine rock looking as solid and homely and familiar as the road along which the car sped.

Visitors usually found this local stone either abysmally ugly or rather interesting, depending on their knowledge of Pennsylvania architecture. Alix, however, made no comment about the house. She was too absorbed by the beauty of the countryside. "I don't see how you could bear to leave!"

This remark was one that only an adult would make, and Mindy felt it required no answer. Give Alix six weeks at the farm, and she would sing quite a different tune. The valley was inviting, the scenery bucolic, but the place was simply too remote to appeal to anyone who was young and vigorous. To argue the point, however, would be futile. "It *is* beautiful," Mindy said sincerely, and found that she was childishly eager to feel the warmth of her parents' welcoming arms.

Both her mother and father looked tanned and hearty, their skin weathered by a lifetime of country living, their eyes glowing with pleasure. "We've missed you!" Mrs. Hubbard confessed, as she held her daughter off and looked at her. "Darling, you're thinner. Are you feeling all right?"

Mindy caught Alix's eye and burst out laughing. "Didn't I tell you? Unless I'm round as a butterball they think I'm ill."

"Come in, come in!" Mr. Hubbard was urging. He had brought the two suitcases from the car and was standing against the screen door to keep it open. "It's much cooler inside."

As usual the kitchen was the room into which everyone entered. The front door was rarely used, because it was approached by a flight of steps, while the back door led from the sloping hill straight into a beam-ceilinged room. Here a modern electric stove faced an old-fashioned walk-in fireplace still hung with antique iron pots on a swinging crane.

"How perfectly marvelous this kitchen is!" Alix cried. "Every time I come here I want to wrap it up and take it home with me."

Her delight was so contagious that Mindy found herself seeing her own home with a fresh eye. The popcorn crocheted bedspread on her four-poster had never seemed exceptional until Alix remarked on it. The tall case clock on the landing had chimes that rang more sweetly because an appreciative ear was listening. The pasture was greener, the hay in the barn more fragrant, the kitchen garden more tempting, all because Alix was here.

"It's fun to have a guest who really enjoys the place," Mrs. Hubbard remarked to Mindy, after Alix had changed to slacks and an old shirt and gone off to inspect the horses with her host. Mindy had lingered behind, because she could sense her mother's need to talk. "Tell me all about everything," Mrs. Hubbard begged. "Do you really like working in the store? Have you met any young people? Is Alix as pleasant to live with as it would appear?"

"Alix is wonderful, simply wonderful," Mindy replied. "She's taught me so much already. You've no idea!" There were so many things to recount that the words tumbled over one another as Mindy sought to describe The Country Cousin, the New York garment district, Jack's apartment, Robin Hood Dell, and the people with whom she worked or played—Paula, Irene, the Scott sisters, Bob Weintraub, Dana Fraser, Laura Goodwin. The only person she avoided mentioning was Peter Knox.

Mrs. Hubbard was the one who brought up his name. "You know Annette and Jack are driving up with Peter tomorrow," she said casually. "I thought instead of Sunday dinner we'd have a picnic lunch out under the trees."

"That sounds nice," Mindy agreed.

Her mother went on planning cheerfully. "I have half a ham, and there should be plenty of strawberries ripe enough to pick."

As Mindy knew, this meant strawberry shortcake

with whipped cream, and she wondered how Alix's powers of resistance would fare when confronted with such country cooking. She herself was determined to be cautious. The pounds she had lost were good riddance. In the long mirror on her closet door she looked positively svelte, and she liked this new image. Perhaps —it was a small perhaps, but one she couldn't help injecting into her thoughts—Peter Knox would like it too.

The next morning she put on a pair of yellow shorts and a clean white shirt, and took a big colander out to the berry patch as soon as the breakfast dishes were finished. Alix, who had taken a wide-brimmed straw hat from a kitchen peg and placed it squarely on her head, joined her. Together they crouched and worked their way down the rows, nipping the sun-warmed strawberries carefully from their stem and placing them gently in the container. Some were too succulent to resist, and they ate them, Mindy a trifle guiltily, Alix with the assurance that such a chance wouldn't come her way often. Then they took their harvest into the kitchen to wash and hull, while Mrs. Hubbard made German potato salad spiked with fresh scallions in a big wooden bowl.

The day was a fine one, warm in the sun, but decently cool in the shade. The arrival of the dinner guests was heralded by an impetuous honking from far down the entrance lane. Jack always used a rhythmic pattern of sound to announce his arrival.

Everyone hurried outside, and for the first few minutes there was a confusion of voices: Annette's high and light, Jack's bubbling with good spirits, Peter's lazy and drawling, as Mindy had remembered it from the wedding reception. She touched Annette's cheek with hers, hugged her brother briefly, and shook Peter's hand. "It's nice to see you again," she said politely, then reintroduced Alix. "I think you've met our cousin, Mrs. Moore."

With her usual social poise, Alix made Peter feel welcome, while the Hubbards quite naturally gathered around the bride and groom. Annette looked radiant—Mindy couldn't help applying the cliché—in a white cotton sundress, and Jack was obviously happy.

"What a day!" he cried. "Made to order!" Rambling around the kitchen, he stole a potato from the salad and a couple of strawberries from the partially filled bowl. Then he and his father led Peter off to inspect a new colt while Annette perched on a kitchen stool and chattered about Bermuda and the fun that snorkeling in the clear blue water of the coral-studded coves had been.

Once more, as on the night in the apartment, Mindy felt her instinctive resistance crumble. Annette was so completely unselfconscious that she was easy to like, and Mindy had learned that her air of assurance was typical of the Philadelphia girls with whom she had grown up. She seemed as at home in this farm kitchen as she did in the rather formal suburban house in which she had always lived, and Mrs. Hubbard at once began to treat her as a member of the family.

When Annette asked, "Is there anything I can do?" she said, "Why, yes. Run out and pick a couple of heads of garden lettuce for lunch. It should be washed and drained between paper towels in the refrigerator to get really crisp."

Half an hour later all the advance preparations were completed, and Jack and Peter had set up a badminton net on the flat strip of lawn between the house and the corral. Annette played as Jack's partner and Mindy as Peter's. Alix begged off, because Mr. Hubbard had saddled two horses and promised to take her for a ride around the farm.

Mindy wasn't surprised that she and Peter were the losers. Neither of them were very athletic, nor did they have Jack's determination to win every game he played. "You're soft!" her brother accused Peter. "It's all this high living and low thinking. Why don't you give up the late nights and get a little exercise?"

Peter grinned lazily. "That's just what I'm planning to do. Anyway, all my playmates have gone to Europe or Cape Cod."

"Even Phyllis?" asked Annette.

Nodding sorrowfully, Peter replied, "I may have to start consoling myself with the younger set." Then he glanced at Mindy so mischievously that she blushed and dropped the badminton bird she was bouncing idly in her hand.

Was he teasing or was he now regarding her with genuine interest? It was hard to tell. She wished she knew how to be provocative, but instead she merely felt uneasy. So uneasy, in fact, that a few minutes later she broke away from the group with the excuse that she must help her mother. "Wait, I'll come with you," Annette suggested, and walked along beside her to the house.

When they were out of earshot of the boys, she said, "Don't let Peter's bored-young-man-about-town pose put you off. Actually, he's not half so blasé as he tries to appear. It's all a front."

"Have you known him long?" Mindy asked.

"Practically forever. We went to nursery school together."

"He's terribly good-looking, isn't he?"

"Terribly," Annette agreed. "It's too bad in a way."

"Why?"

"Because girls have always spoiled him, and he's come to expect it. He leans on admiration like a crutch." Annette frowned. "Somewhere along the line I think

Peter lost a sense of his own identity, which is too bad. He seems much younger than Jack, don't you think?"

Mindy hadn't considered the matter at all, but after a moment she nodded her head. "I guess he does."

"Maybe it's because he's still in college. He didn't have quite enough credits to graduate, so he's going back for a fifth year. And he hasn't a clue about what he wants to do with his life, besides having fun, I mean."

Mindy felt unexpectedly defensive. "Lots of boys don't decide on careers while they're still in school. Not like Jack, I mean. He's always known he wanted to be a doctor."

"Jack's one of the lucky ones."

"Lucky?" Mindy didn't understand. "He's always worked terribly hard."

"I mean lucky because he's motivated, as my father would say. He's got his life in focus. I guess that's what I liked about him, the first night Daddy brought him home for dinner. He was a boy who knew where he was going. And believe me, Mindy, these days that's rare."

Praise of her brother was always enjoyable, but Peter's cause had become important to Mindy. "Sometimes I think Jack is too serious," she said.

"Jack?" Annette positively hooted. "Jack's twice as much fun as Peter! You wait and see."

You wait and see. The words were a promise as well as a warning. They meant that Annette had interpreted the conversation on the badminton court just as Mindy had. Peter was lonely; she was young but available. Maybe he would, eventually, ask her for a date.

This possibility buoyed Mindy up and made her feel more attractive and secure than usual. She stopped worrying about whether her parents would seem countrified to Jack's sophisticated friend, and she stopped being concerned about the crudeness of the heavy pottery and stainless steel with which she and Annette set the trestle table. The yellow-and-white checked cloth was gay, the bowl of larkspur in the center as blue as the sky, and the food was simple but delicious. Alix, back from her ride, looked warm and disheveled and surprisingly young, Jack and Annette were smiling and gay, and even Peter seemed to enter into the spirit of things and enjoy himself. He ate two helpings of fresh strawberry shortcake and claimed that only stern self-discipline made him refuse a third.

After lunch everyone but Mr. and Mrs. Hubbard, who were accustomed to a heavy midday meal, grew sleepy. Alix went to her room to take a nap, Jack and Annette changed to swim suits and went off through the fields to stretch out on the banks of a spring-fed pond, and Peter, yawning, settled himself in the shade with the Sunday newspaper.

Mindy, who had been about to join her brother and his bride, changed her mind and decided to stay around the house. Although a few minutes ago she had been as sleepy as the others, she now pretended to be restless, and decided to take a walk. "Want to come along?" she invited Peter, as she passed him. Asking the question took a lot of courage, but she tried to make it sound unpremeditated.

Peter almost refused. Mindy could tell by the expression of annoyance that momentarily crossed his face. Then he sighed and stood up, stretching. "O.K."

She led him up the slope past the apple orchard and the grove of young pines her father had planted ten years ago, to the brow of a hill that overlooked the long green valley. Here an ancient oak tree spread its long arms over a tumbledown stone wall. The place was quiet, and the view was soothing.

"Quite a spread," commented Peter, leaning on his elbows after he had tested a teetering stone on the wall.

"You can see for more than fifteen miles," Mindy told him. Now that she had him completely to herself she didn't know how to get away from the trivialities of impersonal conversation.

"Years ago I suppose the Chester Valley looked like this. Before the days of the turnpikes and the industrial plants."

"And the motels."

Peter shuddered. "I'm not like Jack," he said unexpectedly. "He believes that change is progress, but I like things the way they were when I was young."

Mindy laughed. "You talk like an old man."

"I talk like a Philadelphian," Peter corrected her. "I don't like to see the big estates broken up and made into housing developments or turned into schools or seminaries or convents." He thrust his chin out, and said very deliberately, "I like our way of life."

"Your way of life or your parents'?" I sound like Jack, Mindy thought, Jack arguing just for the sake of argument. Actually, she had planned to placate Peter, not provoke him. Annoyed with herself, she too pretended to consider the view.

Scowling, Peter asked abruptly, "Why isn't it the same thing?"

"But how can it be? We're just beginning, and—and we've got to earn a view like this." She spread her arms. "Or even a view from a basement apartment, for that matter." Then she broke off and bit her lip. "Oh, I forgot. You're rich."

This seemed to amuse Peter rather than to arouse his indignation. He grinned down at her. "Are you being funny deliberately or just to see how I'll react?"

"Neither," Mindy replied truthfully. "You *are* rich, I think, compared with us."

"Perhaps," Peter admitted, "but it's all relative, you

know. We're poor compared to most of our friends."

"You're talking about your family again, not yourself," Mindy scolded. "We can be anything we want to be, don't you see?"

"Oh sure," said Peter with a shrug. "I can marry a rich girl. And, as a matter of fact, that's just what I plan to do."

Mindy was shocked. "You have to be kidding."

"No, as a matter of fact, I'm completely serious."

"I don't believe you!" Mindy cried. "You're just pretending, because you think you sound—oh, sort of jaded and smart!" She had no right to be talking to Peter this way, and she was appalled at what she was saying, but her tongue was out of control. "I think you're nice. You've grown accustomed to saying things like that simply for effect."

Peter turned and looked at her, really looked at her, his dark eyes taunting, then suddenly gentle. He reached out and took Mindy's hands, which she had unconsciously clenched, and stood looking down at them until she relaxed and let the fingers go slack.

"I think you're nice too," he said. "Very nice. But you've got a lot of growing up to do." Then he sighed, and as though he were flouting his better judgment, said, "Maybe you need an older man in your life. How about going in town for dinner with me some night next week?"

Mindy stood very still, collecting her wits. At the most surprising possible time, just when she was sure she had ruined her chances once and for all, Peter was asking her for a date. She caught her breath and tried not to tremble, but she couldn't help herself, so she pulled her hands away and clasped them behind her back. "What night?" she asked in a whisper, although any night would do.

Peter seemed to consider. "How about Friday?"

"That would be fine."

Fine? The invitation was the most she could have hoped for, in her wildest dreams, and the fact that Friday was nearly a week away only heightened Mindy's anticipation. When Alix rang the old dinner bell, which hung outside the back door, in a prearranged signal that it was time to start back to Saint Davids, Mindy ran down the hill on winged feet. She felt as bright as a bubble, as light as thistledown. And she wanted to shout to all the world that she—she, Mindy Hubbard, the country cousin—had a date with Peter Knox!

Nine

"I've been thinking," said Alix, but Mindy scarcely heard her. She was trying to figure out whether her cousin would let her buy a new dress at the store before next Friday night.

"I said, I've been thinking," Alix repeated, as she drew to a stop at the point where the Yellow Springs road connected with the highway that led through Pottstown toward Philadelphia.

"I'm sorry. I was daydreaming," Mindy apologized. "What were you going to say?"

The car leaped forward once more, and as soon as she had negotiated the turn Alix settled back. "It's good for me to get away for a weekend like this," she commented with a change of approach. "It gives me perspective. And it gives me time to mull over ideas."

Mindy waited, only half listening. If she could buy a dress at cost from The Country Cousin, which one should it be?

"I've been thinking about Paris."

"Paris?" Compared to dinner with Peter in Philadelphia the word seemed like the echo of a dream.

"If it could be done legally, it might be enormous fun and moderately profitable. *If* it would be legal. I have no desire to languish in a French prison, waiting for the American consul to arrange for my release."

Mindy was nonplused. "What *are* you talking about?"

"Selling American clothes in Paris." Alix sounded surprised that there should be any question. "It might be worthwhile to investigate. I could write the Department of Commerce and tell them what I'd like to do. I suppose those people in Washington must know whether such a plan is possible or simply out of the question. From the standpoint of customs, I mean."

"Frankly, I'm lost. Could you start at the beginning, Alix?"

"Certainly. Actually you were the one who gave me the idea. Coming back from New York on the train, remember?"

"But you acted as though it were out of the question."

"I know. But then Mrs. Paige, who came in with her daughter and bought all those clothes, said virtually the same thing. And up at the farm I got to thinking. There's a Mr. André who travels in the United States taking orders for handbags made in France, and American businessmen fly all over the world selling steam turbines and tractors and things. Actually, why shouldn't I sell clothes in Paris?"

Alix glanced at Mindy, but hurried on. "The clothing industry is our seventh largest, and our products are superb. The Germans make fine cameras and microscopes and transistor radios, but their twenty-five-dollar dresses are horrors. French perfumes and French champagne and creations by Dior are incomparable, but it's next to impossible to buy a really well-made inexpensive dress in a French department store."

Mindy was listening more carefully now, but she didn't interrupt, even though Alix was beginning to repeat herself.

"Take our drip-dry cottons, and our John Meyer skirts and sweaters. Take any of the Craely clothes I had with me when I went to Paris. Why, if the French girls knew how little they cost, they'd—they'd—"

"They'd flip," Mindy supplied.

"Right. Take that dress you have on. How much did it cost?"

"I made it myself."

"Did you really?" Alix sounded surprised. "It's a very nice dress! But what I'm trying to say is that we're tops in the field of ready-to-wear. A thirty-dollar dress from the United States is something for which a well-brought-up French girl might quite happily sell her soul."

Mindy laughed. She had never heard Alix make a soap-box oration before, and to find that she could be so carried away was amusing. "You mean that if you should take a collection of clothes from The Country Cousin to Paris the French as well as the Americans might be interested?"

"It's conceivable," replied Alix more cautiously.

"Then what's the problem?"

"The problem is: can it be done?"

"But if Mr. André sells French handbags over here—"

"The Americans are much more easygoing than the French, yet even Mr. André has to bring his samples into the country in bond."

"In bond? What's that?"

"He has to post a bond, put up a certain amount of money, in order to bring in samples without paying duty. Then when he leaves the United States to go home, the customs officers check over his cases to make sure he's going out with precisely the same items he brought in."

"Do the French do things the same way?"

"I should think not!" Alix said with a laugh. "The French always make things twice as complicated as we do. It's part of the national policy."

"My, knowing another country the way you do would be marvelous," Mindy said, sighing.

"Know France? Why, darling, I haven't even

scratched the surface. To know France would take a lifetime. But I must say I enjoyed my small taste of Paris. That's why I'd love to go back."

"Then why *don't* you write the Department of Commerce, the way you suggested? It wouldn't hurt to ask."

"It wouldn't hurt to ask," Alix repeated slowly and thoughtfully. "I think I'll invest a five-cent stamp and do just that."

Thereafter the subject was dropped, because traffic became heavier with every passing mile and Alix began to concentrate on her driving. Mindy fell asleep in her corner of the front seat and dozed until they had passed Valley Forge. She was aroused by her cousin saying, "So you made that dress yourself? Since I can't sew a stitch I'm quite impressed."

"I don't really like to sew," Mindy confessed, "but I love to work out ideas for clothes. I remember—when I was quite young, not more than twelve, I suppose—pouring over old copies of *Vogue* in the dentist's office. Mother has a sewing machine, and during the summers I used to buy cotton materials in the village and follow patterns. Then after a while the patterns didn't suit me, so I tried making my own. Of course, I've never made anything half so pretty as the dresses at The Country Cousin."

Alix didn't contradict her. Instead, she asked, "How did you start making a pattern of your own?"

"Well, first I'd do a little sketch of the way I wanted the dress to look. I've always liked to draw, you see. You were looking at some of the things on my bedroom walls."

"Were they yours, Mindy? I hadn't realized! The watercolor of the barn, and the pen and ink of the grazing cattle? They're quite charming."

Such flattery was so unprecedented that Mindy felt embarrassed. "I'm afraid art was my only good subject."

Alix ignored this explanation. "So you made the sketch. Then what?"

"Then I worked the lines out in a paper pattern that would fit me. You get to know your own size pretty well after a few attempts."

"I'm fascinated," said Alix. "Truly I am. Why didn't you ever tell me about any of this?"

Mindy shrugged. "It didn't seem important. Home-made clothes would seem silly to the girls around here."

"Mindy, Mindy!" Alix said with a sigh. "You should be proud of yourself, not apologetic. There isn't a girl your age who comes into The Country Cousin who wouldn't brag about being able to make a dress like the one you have on."

After they reached Saint Davids and had carried their suitcases to the second floor, Alix came into Mindy's bedroom and asked to be shown the other dresses she had designed and made herself. Turning them inside out to inspect the seams and the linings, she made little clucks of approval. "You've done a really good job."

But such praise wasn't music to Mindy's ears at this particular moment. She had returned to thinking about the coming Friday night, and suddenly she could contain herself no longer. "Peter Knox has asked me to go out to dinner next weekend," she told Alix. "My month isn't up until Thursday the sixteenth, but could you possibly let me buy a new dress before then?"

Her earnestness apparently touched as well as amused Alix. "I think we could stretch a point," she said.

"Oh, thank you!" Mindy sounded as rapturous as she felt. Spontaneously she went over and hugged her cousin. "Oh, thank you very much!"

Anticipation always heightened Mindy's color and made her eyes sparkle, so during the next week, whenever she looked into the long mirrors at the store, she saw a girl who was prettier than the one who had so recently left to spend the Fourth of July weekend at the farm. She felt full of vitality, which she communicated not only to Alix's assistants, but to the customers she served. No longer did she tend to oversell, but her obvious delight in the clothes she showed was enough to convince many shoppers.

Concerning the choice of a dress for herself, however, Mindy dillydallied. The red linen had long since been sold, but the white was still available, and there was a new skimmer in a shade called lemon ice that looked almost as smart as white with her deepening tan.

Finally, unable to come to a decision, she put the choice up to Alix. "Which do you like?"

"The white," said Alix at once. "You should wear white often, Mindy. It's very becoming."

"But for dinner in Philadelphia?"

Alix leaned against the doorway to the fitting room. "Never buy a dress for a single occasion," she warned. "That's no way to build a useful wardrobe."

"Well—" Mindy regarded herself critically. "All right, if you say so."

Alix smiled and patted her young cousin's shoulder. "Trust me," she said. "I'm sure you won't be sorry."

Mindy certainly wasn't sorry when she was ready to go out on Friday night. Her hair was shining, her short white gloves spanking clean, her nail polish fresh. The new white dress touched her body as lightly as a feather, and, as Alix had promised, she felt precisely right.

Peter arrived fifteen minutes after the time he had suggested, which wasn't surprising. Mindy shrewdly suspected he was a lad who let girls wait for him as a matter of course.

The car he was driving was a far cry from the bucket-seated convertible Mindy had envisioned. It was a

Chevrolet, neither new enough to be modish nor ancient enough to be considered vintage, and it started with a cough and a sputter that evoked no great sense of confidence.

Even Peter seemed a little mistrustful. "But at any rate it's better than a motorcycle," he said, as they headed toward the expressway. He made no comment on Mindy's appearance, and this omission was a trifle disappointing when she had worked so hard over the total effect, but perhaps he was too concerned with the car's performance to be aware of anything else.

At least, Mindy consoled herself with this reasoning. In any case, simply being there beside him, with the sun setting in the west and the reflection forming a backdrop for the Philadelphia skyline should have been enough. "I thought we'd go down to the waterfront," Peter said, "where there's a restaurant called 1700 that's built on a pier. We can sit close to the river and watch the boats pass. It's sort of fun."

Mindy agreed happily, as she would have agreed to anything that Peter proposed. However, the riverside section to which they soon came seemed anything but glamorous. Warehouses nudged one another along a street that was broad but abandoned and dreary at this time of night, and when Peter turned through narrow gates into a big parking lot there was still no indication that anything especially interesting was in store. Then

Mindy raised her eyes just as the lights illuminating a ship flashed on. It was a big schooner, placed alongside the pier, whose four masts rose tall against the darkening sky.

"Oh, look!" she gasped, immediately intrigued.

Peter seemed amused by her spontaneous reaction. "I always manage to have them put on the lights just as I arrive," he teased.

"Is it floating there?"

Peter shook his head. "She's in drydock. She came over under full sail, manned by Swedish sailors, but I don't suppose she'll ever float again."

"Can we go aboard?" Mindy asked.

"Oh sure. As a matter of fact, we can sit on deck and have a coke before we go in to dinner."

This proposal delighted Mindy. She thought Peter was very clever to have arranged such an exciting— even romantic—evening, and she was prepared to enjoy every moment of it.

The schooner, named the *Sonja*, was approached by a gangplank leading up from a square paved with Belgian blocks and lined with replicas of eighteenth-century shops. With an authority Mindy found impressive in a young man of his age, Peter led Mindy aboard and found a small table, situated, as he had promised, on the deck overlooking the river. "This is marvelous!" she breathed.

"It's a tourist trap, actually, but I thought you might enjoy it."

"I don't see why you call it a tourist trap. I think it's perfectly fascinating."

A waiter in a pre-Revolutionary costume came and took their order, while on the river a big freighter escorted by a tugboat steamed slowly toward the sea. Mindy jumped, startled, when a horn hooted loudly. "Where was that?"

"At the restaurant, right next door," Peter said. "The management plays games with passing ships, and sometimes one blows its horn in acknowledgment. There! Like that."

Mindy clasped her hands and smiled. She felt as though Peter had arranged every effect for her special entertainment: the lights of the great factories across the river in Camden, the glowing arc of the Walt Whitman Bridge, even the Delaware River traffic itself. She could have been a million miles away from Bryn Mawr and Saint Davids, not a mere seventeen.

Their drinks finished, Peter didn't linger. "I'm hungry," he said. "Besides, I made reservations for eight o'clock."

Back down the gangplank they walked, past the small-paned windows of half a dozen tempting shops, and into a dimly lighted tavern on the river's edge. A head-waiter led them to a table, handed them enormous menus, and after they had ordered Mindy kept up a running conversation about the restaurant, asking Peter questions and "ohing" and "ahing" in such a complimentary fashion that she could see he was pleased. But in time, of course, the subject was exhausted, and then Mindy was at a loss.

The thought occurred to her that she knew practically nothing about this friend of her brother's. She had danced with him once, rather disastrously, and had been alone with him only for about fifteen minutes last Sunday at the farm. What were his interests? She searched her mind belatedly. Tennis. Girls. "Do you play much tennis?" she essayed.

"Not what you'd call a lot. Couple of times a week."

"I've been playing a little with Laura Goodwin."

"Laura?" This name seemed to disturb Peter. "Isn't she an awful dud?"

"I don't think so. But then, I'm not very good myself."

"I didn't mean that. I mean Laura's not exactly— well, not sort of with it, not very hep."

"Isn't she?" Mindy felt ill at ease. "I think she seems quite nice."

"Well, maybe to another girl."

Mindy buttered a hot popover and dropped the subject, which appeared to have reached a dead end. She didn't quite know what was expected, but since Peter didn't seem about to initiate any new topic of conversation, she decided to try again.

"Does Phyllis play a good game of tennis?" she asked ineptly.

Peter smiled reminiscently. "She talks a good game."

This remark, absurdly enough, put Mindy at a disadvantage, as though Peter had implied that her attempts at conversation were dull. And she was beginning to feel as though he might be right.

Again there was an uncomfortable silence from which Mindy was rescued only by the return of a waiter with more hot popovers. She took a second against her better judgment, and said, "Thank you," with a strained smile.

Peter, meanwhile, was glancing around at the other tables near them, and suddenly he grinned and signaled to someone out of sight behind Mindy's back. In a moment he put his napkin on the table. "Will you excuse me," he asked as a statement rather than a question. "I'd like to go and speak to some people I know."

"Of course."

"I'll be right back." Peter hurried away, his handsome face beaming with animation, and Mindy could hear his voice raised in greeting. "Mrs. Carstairs! How do you do, Mr. Carstairs. Hi, Lynn, how was Ireland? When did you get back?"

Mindy privately begged her head not to swivel around and glance behind her, but she couldn't keep it under control. The group at the nearby table was, fortunately, quite unaware of her curiosity. A girl of perhaps nineteen was gazing up at Peter with round gray eyes as he hovered over the table. She was wearing a navy-blue linen dress that wasn't particularly distinguished, but her hair was dressed in the latest style, and it was a Titian red.

Mindy's head turned back again, and she addressed herself to the food as though she were suddenly hungry, although every mouthful was an effort to swallow. Something told her—some sixth sense she could trust as unerringly as she could trust her own mother—that these people were the sort Peter belonged with, that with her he was only filling in time.

Yet something had attracted him that afternoon at the farm. Her unexpected honesty? Her inexperience? Or just the fact that she was Jack's kid sister, who needed to be showed around.

In any event, the attraction had been short-lived. When Peter came back to the table he was talkative in a rather affected manner, but it was the Carstairs he talked about. He described their estate on Mill Creek Road (their "place" he called it, but Mindy could tell that it was huge). He recounted an amusing experience on the night of Lynn's coming-out party, for which a dance floor had been set up on the lawn under a marquee and the champagne had been imported. "Not that cheap American stuff."

Mindy chuckled, and admitted, "I wouldn't know the difference," but such naïveté no longer amused Peter. He kept glancing sideways at Lynn surreptitiously and began to treat Mindy in a patronizing manner.

Little by little, she retreated into an embarrassed silence, locked in a cell from which there was no escape. She managed to smile from time to time at some remark intended to be witty, but she scarcely heard what Peter was saying, and for the first time in her life she was attacked by a wave of jealousy that threatened to choke her. No longer could she pretend to be hungry. When Peter ordered dessert, she said, "Just coffee, thank you," then realized from the expression on her escort's face that for the first time that evening she had done something properly sophisticated.

After another endless interval Peter was presented with a check, which he studied with such concentration that Mindy began to wonder whether he was perhaps short of money. But then he paid it high-handedly, left a tip from the change returned by the waiter, and asked, "Ready, Melinda? Let's go."

In the street of eighteenth-century replicas he no longer seemed interested. Barely pausing at the wooden stock that had been set up in the tiny square, he said, "Sure, Joe Bloke from Punxsutawney thinks gimmicks like this are great, but I think they're for the birds."

When Mindy paused to peer into a candle shop, he hurried her along unceremoniously and didn't try to hide a yawn. "I'm sleepy," he said, more in explanation than apology. "And I've got to get up early tomorrow morning."

"Oh, do you have a summer job?"

"No job, just an early match at the Cricket Club."

"Oh." As in a crystal ball Mindy could see clipped green grass, a net, and a red-haired girl.

"I was going to suggest a *discotheque*, but then I remembered you aren't very keen on dancing."

In the darkness Mindy flushed and bit her lip. He's thinking of the way I stumbled all over his feet at the wedding reception. She also knew that in spite of any effort she might make the evening was irretrievably ruined.

And how could she reply to such a remark? Say, "I love to dance, actually, but I don't know many of the new steps." This answer would be the truth, but it would put her at an even greater disadvantage. "You have a very good memory," she murmured instead, and she couldn't help sounding disgruntled. She was.

Fortunately, the darkness acted as an ally on the ride back to Saint Davids. Mindy turned her face away from the glare of oncoming headlights and yawned once or twice, conspicuously, so that Peter would not feel that he alone was overcome by ennui. Actually, she had never felt more awake or more wretched. She sat curled in the seat in mute misery, the skirt of the white dress crumpled, and wished she had never let herself believe that she could possibly entertain a boy as worldly-wise as Peter Knox.

Peter wasn't the one she blamed. Oh no! She blamed herself. If only she had been born and brought up on the Main Line instead of near a hick town in the Oley Valley. If only she had gone to a dancing class where they taught something up to date instead of the fox trot and the waltz. If only she had something to say! Something bright and witty and nonchalant. If only she weren't such an utter, utter dope.

Hands clutched in her lap, Mindy all but prayed for deliverance, and when Peter finally pulled up in Alix's drive she was out of the car before he could get around to open the door. Artificially, she smiled. Artificially, she thanked him for a lovely dinner. A few hours earlier she had been hoping the evening would end with a romantic interlude. The memory shamed her. All she wanted now was sanctuary, the sanctuary of her own room.

There was a light in the downstairs hall, and another light traced a line under the closed door of her cousin's bedroom. Mindy, slippers in hand, tried to tiptoe past unheard, but Alix called brightly, "Hi, Mindy, back so early? Did you have a good time, dear?"

"Marvelous, just marvelous!" Mindy hoped her voice sounded breathless and joyful instead of pitched artificially high in order to ward off imminent tears. "Good night."

"Good night," Alix called back cheerfully. "By the way, a letter for you got mixed in with my mail. I left it on the bureau in your room."

Mindy couldn't trust herself to say thank you, so she pretended she hadn't heard and let the door shut behind her noisily. Then, still fighting for self-control, she dropped her slippers on the floor, threw her purse and gloves in the direction of the bed, and automatically picked up the envelope on the dresser.

It contained a typewritten letter politely regretting that in view of the large number of candidates and the standard of scholarship demanded, the registrar of the third and last college to which she had applied had been unavoidably delayed in informing Miss Melinda Hubbard that—

Mindy crumpled the letter viciously into a ball and hurled it at the wall. The answer, naturally, was no.

Ten

Between the July sale, which was still bringing more customers than usual to The Country Cousin, and her own renewed feeling of inadequacy, honed to a fine edge by the catastrophe of Friday evening, Mindy was so busy with her own concerns that she scarcely noticed her cousin's preoccupation with a sheaf of literature received from the United States Department of Commerce in Washington. For the better part of the following week booklets, pamphlets, and mimeographed papers lay on the coffee table. Then one evening, after poring over them for an hour, Alix gathered them up and marched to the kitchen wastebasket. "Nothing at all that pertains to my situation," she said, as she dumped them in.

Mindy, who was turning the pages of a new *Vogue* and thinking that by middle age salesgirls' feet must ache continuously, glanced up. "Somebody," said her cousin firmly, "must know something about taking commercial samples to Europe. I'm going to get an appointment with the head of the foreign department of the First Pennsylvania Company."

Forthwith she drove in to Philadelphia, leaving the store in Irene's charge during a particularly busy afternoon. She returned, none the wiser, but with a new glint of determination in her eye. "Imagine!" she said to Mindy. "The best bank in the city, and all they can do is to suggest I write the French consulate in New York!"

This letter went off that very evening, and a reply came four days later. "We advise that you contact the American Chamber of Commerce in Paris concerning this rather unusual question."

Alix followed the advice, writing airmail, and after a typical July heat wave had come and gone she received an answer that once more sent the temperature in Saint Davids soaring. "We suggest, madam, that you get in touch with the French consul in New York, who will undoubtedly be able to apprise you of the current rulings. At the same time you might be wise to contact the Department of Commerce in Washington. We are in no position to enter into a discussion of the proposition you suggest."

"Now I know what people mean when they say they're getting the runaround," Alix said to Mindy.

"Here I am, right back where I started nearly a month ago."

"Maybe you'd better give up the whole thing."

Alix shook her head. "Not yet. Mrs. Paige knows the French consul in Philadelphia. I think I'll try to get an appointment with him in person. Maybe letters like mine never get to the higher-ups. Maybe some junior clerk types out routine answers, simply designed to be discouraging."

On the day that she was to visit the consul Alix dressed with special care and came to Mindy for inspection. "Will I pass?"

"You look perfectly lovely!"

"But do I look smart?"

"To me you do."

Alix sighed. "Thank you, darling. But passing muster with a Frenchman will be something else again." She blew a mock kiss. "*Au revoir*, and wish me luck."

The realization that even Mrs. Moore—adult, intrepid, and the owner of an up-and-coming business—still had her moments of insecurity was a comfort, in a fashion. By closing time Alix hadn't returned, so Paula drove Mindy home and suggested, "Better get something started for supper. Mrs. Moore will have put in a long day. She's going to be tired."

Willingly, Mindy set to work. She opened a can of King crab, sliced a cucumber, and made a salad that would keep cool in the refrigerator. Then she took a carton of French-fried eggplant from the freezer, got it ready to pop into the oven, and made a pitcher of iced tea flavored with fresh garden mint. The house was hot and stuffy, so she set a table on the terrace with straw mats and paper napkins. Still Alix hadn't arrived, and the clock hands had reached six forty-five.

When she did come in, a little after seven, she looked wilted and furious. "He kept me waiting an hour and twenty minutes, and then guess what he said! 'I can't imagine anyone being so foolhardy as to want to sell American clothes in France.' You should have seen his expression: utter horror. You should have heard his voice!"

"Oh, Alix, I *am* sorry!" By this time, Mindy realized, the idea she had presented so innocently that night on the train had attained the proportions of a crusade.

"He was so condescending!" Alix raged. " 'My dear young lady,' he kept saying, 'French clothes are so much better made than any others! Why, my wife bought a dress at Philadelphia's best department store, and the first time she wore it the seam surrounding the —the how-do-you-say?—zipper split three inches, so that she was compelled to excuse herself from a diplomatic reception.' "

Alix was such a good mimic that Mindy burst out laughing. "What did you say to that?"

" 'How unfortunate, *m'sieur*, but even the seam on a Dior has been known to come unsewed.' "

"Good for you!"

Alix managed a rueful grin. "That was my only inning. From five thirty until six fifteen I was lectured on the glories of French couture. Then the gentleman informed me that he was a political and cultural consul, but not a commercial one, so that in any case I had brought my case to the wrong court."

"Did he have anything helpful to suggest?"

"Oh, yes." Alix ran her fingers through her hair wearily. "He patted my shoulder and told me that if I really insisted on pursuing the matter, I should try the French consul general in New York."

"But you already have, haven't you?"

Alix nodded. "I feel like a kitten chasing my tail. Of course, he also suggested that I write our Department of Commerce."

"Like a kitten chasing *two* tails," murmured Mindy sympathetically. "Let's have some supper. I've set the table out on the terrace, and maybe you'll feel better after you've had something to eat."

But Alix only felt more indignant as the evening wore on. In spite of the heat she went upstairs and wrote a second, peremptory letter to the American Chamber of Commerce in Paris asking for specific information on three itemized questions. This one she read aloud to

Mindy, then walked a quarter of a mile down the road to mail it. "Now," she said upon her return, "we'll see."

There followed an interval of comparative peace and quiet during which Mindy tried to pull herself together and tackle her own problems. She'd make a determined effort to put Peter out of her mind; he was too old for her anyway. As for the letter from the registrar, she had half expected it. Most of the girls in her class had received a reply in response to their applications before school closed. Furthermore, the high-school principal had not been sanguine concerning her chances, reminding her that competition these days was increasingly stiff.

The future seemed to yawn like a pit in a James Bond movie, threatening to engulf her if she made one more misstep. The summer was taken care of, because in spite of the fact that her social life had come to a standstill, Mindy enjoyed her work at The Country Cousin more than ever. And she tried not to think about what might happen to her in the fall.

"There's always secretarial school," her mother wrote comfortingly from the farm, but Mindy shuddered at the thought of spending eight dreary hours each day hunched over a desk in Reading, Pennsylvania. I won't, she promised herself. I'll find something better to do!

In the meantime, Laura Goodwin had left with her

parents for a month on Mount Desert Island, Jack and Annette had both found part-time jobs that kept them so busy they had no time for entertaining, and Dana Fraser was apparently occupied with other concerns. In order to fill her evenings Mindy was thrown back on her own resources, so she consoled herself in the manner to which she had become accustomed. She bought some lovely tissue-wool material and started to make a dress.

Alix seemed relieved to find her young charge thus occupied. She was so busy herself that idleness in another person seemed a waste. This attitude Mindy could sense, as she could also sense her cousin's tacit understanding that Peter Knox was no longer in the picture. She neither asked unanswerable questions nor did she try to commiserate.

Besides, she was launched on an engrossing game. From the American Chamber of Commerce in Paris Alix had learned, finally, that she could indeed take a collection of sample clothes to France under an arrangement called *Admission Temporaire*.

"I wouldn't be allowed to sell any of the models, but I could take orders on them. Then I'd have to reship the entire collection to the United States."

"Would that be worthwhile?" Mindy asked.

Her cousin shrugged. "This fellow doesn't seem to think so. He says, 'Such a venture could scarcely be profitable, since we know of no American firm who tries to sell clothes in this manner.' " Alix looked up and wrinkled her nose. "Meaning in a hotel room," she interpolated. "That's not quite true, because I've read in *Women's Wear Daily* that lots of French firms show their samples in hotel rooms. Why do people have to be so balky about something that's a new idea to them?"

Mindy had no answer for this or for any of the other rhetorical questions that Alix posed. But as correspondence began to fly back and forth from Saint Davids to all sorts of official-sounding offices, and bit by bit pieces of the jigsaw puzzle on which her cousin was working fell into place, she became captivated with the game.

She also acted as Mrs. Moore's sounding board. "Perhaps my idea is too simple for everyone," Alix said one evening, when they were driving back from an air-conditioned movie in Ardmore. "I just want to show my dresses, take orders, collect payment and postage, and mail them off to the customers from Bryn Mawr. You'd think, when the head of the World Bank makes a speech telling businessmen that the United States government wants small business to trade abroad, somebody would know how to manage to do just that."

"Maybe," said Mindy soothingly, "he didn't have quite such a *small* business in mind."

Alix burst out laughing. "*Touché.*" Then she turned serious. "But you know something, Mindy? In the past few days I've had a feeling that I'm on my way. Take the things we're now sure of: I *won't* have to pay taxes or duty. I *can* show my samples. It's not usual to rent a hotel suite in Paris as a place to take orders, but it's not impossible."

"Is there anything else you really need to know."

"That's just it. I don't know what I don't know. Maybe I never will until I get there."

"Then you really are going?"

"I hope so."

"Goodness! When?"

"I'd like to leave on Labor Day."

"*This* Labor Day? Why, that's less than a month away." For the first time the project became more than a puzzle to Mindy. Because her own prospects for fall looked so dreary, her cousin's seemed incredibly exciting. "Paris!" she breathed. "Oh, Alix, I don't see how you can sleep nights. I really don't."

Alix smiled. " 'There is many a slip. . . .' " she started to quote. "But I am sure of one thing. The wholesalers will cooperate. They all think it's a nifty idea."

"Then you've talked to them about it?"

"Oh, yes. I had lunch with Harvey Weintraub again last week, and he feels sure I can swing it. He keeps insisting, though, that it's too much to handle alone. He wants me to take along some help."

"Like Paula?"

Alix shook her head. "I'd have to leave Paula and

Irene in charge of the store. And I don't see how I could choose between the Scott girls."

"Then—" Suddenly a marvelous possibility dawned on Mindy. Her eyes widened and her eyebrows rose. "Then who?" The expression on her cousin's face made her bolder. "Not me?"

Alix nodded. "I thought you must have guessed, but I didn't want to get your hopes up until—"

Mindy never heard the rest of the sentence. She sat absolutely still, in a state of shock so intense that she felt as though to move a muscle would be to shatter into a thousand pieces. She, Melinda Hubbard, going to Paris? She, Melinda Hubbard, who had never been farther afield than Philadelphia and New York? She would see the Eiffel Tower, the Champs Élysées, Notre Dame, Montmartre, all of the places she knew only from pictures? No, it couldn't happen. It was too unbelievable.

"You see," Alix was saying, "something could still go wrong. It's not anything to count on positively, Mindy, but I couldn't wait any longer to tell you, because I'm so excited myself I want to share it with somebody. And I think to take you would be the obvious solution. Besides, we'd have fun!"

"Fun?" Mindy, who rarely cried, could feel the tears slipping down her face. "Fun? Why, Alix, it would be the most wonderful experience in my whole life!"

"Oh, darling, this was what I was afraid of!" Alix sounded distressed. "Mindy, you mustn't count on it too much! A dozen things could happen that would make the trip impossible."

"I know," Mindy sniffled. "I'll try not to. But, oh Alix, wouldn't it be heavenly, wouldn't it be absolutely heavenly, to see Paris with you?"

"We'd be working most of the time," Alix warned. "We'd have our evenings, and Sundays of course, but during the day we'd be open for business from nine thirty to five o'clock."

"Even so—" Mindy drew a long, tremulous breath of anticipation. "I just can't believe it. I just can't."

"Good," said Alix with down-to-earth practicality. "Hold on to that point of view until we're over the Atlantic."

"Oh, would we fly?" This prospect made Mindy positively shivery.

"Of course. I couldn't spare the time to go by boat. You see, besides everything else, I've got to make this venture pay. We've got to sell enough clothes to make our expenses and some more besides. Otherwise the trip would be quite unjustified."

But Mindy at this point refused to let business intrude on romance. She sat, spellbound with excitement, until Alix said, "We're home, pet. Do you plan to get out of the car or to sleep here all night?"

Eleven

For the next several days Mindy felt as though she were suspended above the earth in a balloon. The strings were controlled by those mysterious men in Washington with whom Alix corresponded, and sometimes the balloon tipped precariously, but she hadn't fallen out yet.

On another level, in her real life, Mindy began to read everything about Paris she could find. Alix had a big book of photographs of the city, and the library had many more. Mindy even read a book on French cooking, so that she would know what to order in a restaurant. One afternoon she saw Peter pass on the street outside The Country Cousin window and felt scarcely a tremor, her spirits were so high.

Then, on a Wednesday afternoon, she and Alix arrived home from the store and found a letter with the French Embassy seal on it.

"We suggest," wrote an attaché, "that you become a member of the International Salon of Ladies' Wholesalers. Moreover, it seems that any foreigner who performs a commercial activity in France must apply for a Commercial Card."

This requirement didn't seem especially upsetting to Mindy, but for her cousin it was a crushing blow. "Knowing the French," she wailed, "this is bound to take forever. And by forever I mean six months at the very least. I'm going to write the French ambassador himself and make a plea for emergency expediting, but I have little faith my letter will do any good."

In the meantime, Alix had made reservations at a hotel near the Étoile and had placed a small advertisement in the public notices section of the *Paris Tribune*. Within four days of the ad's appearance enthusiastic letters bearing foreign postmarks began to arrive in Bryn Mawr. A woman from Brussels planned to make a special trip to Paris to buy several sweaters and skirts from The Country Cousin. A girl at school in Geneva asked if she could order Villagers by mail. A woman's club in Frankfurt suggested to Alix that if she'd come there as well as to Paris they would put on a fashion show. The French ambassador, however, was incommunicative.

By the first of August Alix was becoming seriously worried. She had received a letter from the French commercial consul saying, "In your own interest, I recommend that you alter your plans and visit France like an ordinary tourist." There was still no news concerning the availability of a Commercial Card.

Naturally Mindy magnified her cousin's concern and made it her own. "Isn't there somebody else we could write to?" she asked.

Alix shook her head in discouragement. "I'll talk to Mr. Weintraub when I go to New York tomorrow," she decided. Then she suggested to Mindy, as though she were tossing a meatless bone to a hungry dog, "Why don't you come along?"

The first visit to the market had whetted Mindy's appetite. Her eyes sparkled, and she replied, "I'd love to." With a newly developed sense of responsibility, however, she added, "But that will leave Beth and Jane alone in the store."

"I'll call Paula and ask if she'll come in for an extra day," Alix proposed. She came back from the telephone with an affirmative answer. "We're all set."

During the night there was a violent thunderstorm, bringing unusually cool air in its wake. "It's more like September than early August," Alix commented, as she and Mindy ate a hurried breakfast in their dressing gowns. "Better wear something warm."

Mindy wanted to oblige, but all she had was the tissue wool she had just finished, and she put it on reluctantly. Appearing in the New York market in a home-made dress didn't seem proper. Alix, however, complimented her on her appearance. "The lines of that skirt are exactly right," she praised.

The train trip, now familiar, seemed far shorter than before, and the walk up Seventh Avenue even more interesting. Winter furs were being carried back and forth, the skins draped over errand boys' arms or the finished coats, protected with plastic coverings, swaying on racks. The dresses on the carts were woolens, dark silks, or long evening gowns, also designed for winter wear. They gave Mindy an understanding of Alix's fear that summer was passing far too fast and that they might be left behind in this frantic race against time.

Walking along purposefully, Alix was absorbed by her own thoughts and apparently oblivious to the passing scene. Mindy, following her, ducked past a cart of children's dresses as bright as flowers and stopped to stare at a quantity of naked display models peering out from behind the glass windows of a ground-floor store. Some of them, made of flesh-toned plastic or papier-mâché, were enough to give the uninitiated a start, but others were an unearthly silver color and looked as though they had just fallen from the moon.

As planned, Alix went first to seek out Harvey Weintraub, who greeted her affectionately. Then he turned to Mindy. "And how is the little one? What a pretty dress you have on, dear. Who made it?"

Mindy caught her cousin's eye and tried to signal by shaking her head, but Alix ignored her. "She made it herself, Harvey, and designed it too. Take a better look."

Mr. Weintraub did so. He took Mindy by the hands and turned her around, then stepped back admiringly. "Come now! You're kidding an old man."

"No, honestly, Harvey."

Mindy flushed and didn't speak.

"You used a pattern. Now tell me the truth."

"It isn't anything," Mindy murmured. "It's very simple. You can see."

"That's what we like around here, simplicity. Simplicity and wearability. Walk across the room, dearie, and let me see how it moves."

Mindy did as she was told, although she felt increasingly awkward. "Very, very nice. You know, Alix, I might even be able to fit it into my line of spring wools."

Alix didn't seem to think this suggestion as astonishing as Mindy did. "We can talk about that later," she said briskly, "but right now I need some advice."

She told him about her problem with the elusive Commercial Card, and he nodded understandingly. "Let me make a phone call to a man I know in the World Bank." After about ten minutes he came back with the address of still another person, in the Department of Commerce, who might be helpful. "But just to be on the safe side he thinks you should also write the Minister of Finance in France."

Mindy stifled a sigh as she thought of the stack of correspondence on her cousin's desk, but Alix was as courteous and appreciative as though time were not running out and two more letters explaining her problems were a mere nothing.

Mr. Weintraub then turned to a discussion of some of the firm's clothes that might prove popular in Europe, and Mindy stayed sedately in the background, listening, until Bob came sauntering in from the cutting room. "I hear you're going to France!" he said.

Alix held up a hand with two crossed fingers, but Mr. Weintraub said, "Now, now, you're practically on your way."

"I wish I could believe it," said Alix late that night, after she had typed and mailed the letters to Washington and Paris. She checked off the date on a wall calendar hanging in the kitchen and went to the refrigerator for a glass of milk.

At the counter top Mindy was wrapping the dress she had designed, which she had sponged and pressed after coming home, in a sturdy box. She was sending it off only because she had promised. "This makes me feel silly," she complained.

Alix turned, milk bottle in hand. "Why is it," she

wondered aloud, "that people tend to discount the very things they do best? If Mr. Weintraub should decide to use that design, Mindy, you might get a nice little check. It would come in handy if we ever *do* get to Paris."

"You mean he'd *pay* me for it?"

"Of course."

"Well!" This was a real surprise.

"That doesn't mean anything," Alix cautioned hastily, "except that you'd have a very lucky break. But I've been wondering, Mindy, whether you've ever thought of going to art school, instead of college, and taking up fashion design?"

"Do you think I could?"

"Why not? There's the Museum School and Moore in Philadelphia, and there must be half a dozen or so in New York."

"I'll have to think about it," Mindy said slowly, recalling Bob Weintraub's previous suggestion. Tonight, however, she was too exhausted to consider such a major step seriously. She trudged upstairs and flung herself across the bed, asleep before she even remembered to call good night.

Ten days passed, ten muggy August days during which business fell off and the girls busied themselves unpacking and ticketing fall woolens. The store was air-conditioned, but even so the materials felt heavy and sticky and unappealing. On the layaway rack Alix reserved a special section where she hung the models she planned to take to Paris, but as the days dragged on and no replies came to any of her more recent letters she became uncharacteristically nervous and irritable.

Finally, on a ninety-degree morning when there had been only one desultory customer, she picked up the telephone grimly and placed a call person-to-person to the National Export Expansion Coordinator in the Department of Commerce. Mindy listened in the background.

"This is Mrs. Moore, Alix Moore," she said sweetly, when the secretary apparently asked who was calling. There was no mention of The Country Cousin. By her ladylike tone one would have thought she was a personal friend.

And when she got the gentleman on the other end of the line she really pulled out all stops. Because Alix was usually such a controlled person, Mindy was astonished to find that she could cajole, plead, and in general behave like an accomplished actress. In the end she managed to elicit some sort of promise. "Well," she said, when she had hung up, "let's hope that gets results."

It did. The next day an employee of the Department of Commerce phoned and assured Mrs. Moore that she could take samples into France in bond and that she wouldn't need a Commercial Card at all. But not until a confirmation came by slow boat in a modest brown paper envelope from the *Ministère des Finances et des Affaires Economiques, Direction des Affaires Commerciales* that Alix quite allowed herself to believe it.

"No office with such a long name could be anything but official!" she crowed with sudden elation. "I can't stay more than three months and I can't make direct sales, which I knew anyway. Whoopee, we're legal at last!"

The excitement that Mindy had tried so unsuccessfully to keep under control was now unleashed. In fact, everyone at The Country Cousin shared in Mrs. Moore's relief and anticipation. Long consultations were held on the final selection of samples. Mindy and the Scott girls were called on to model the numbers in their size, while Irene, Paula, and Alix considered each one critically.

This dress might be too American, that one too conservative to appeal to the style-conscious French. Yet the French probably would not do most of the buying. What would Americans living abroad need and want?

Questions were asked and opinions traded until a final selection was made and a group of outfits were ready to pack in the two large suitcases Alix had bought. Meanwhile, Mindy had to cross several hurdles of her own.

She chose an evening when she was alone in the house to phone her parents and ask for permission to go to France with her cousin. Her mother proved extremely reluctant, which appalled her.

"If you were going by boat, that would be a different matter altogether. But flying—well, I just don't like it, that's all!"

"But Mother," Mindy wailed, "jets are safer than automobiles. There are all sorts of statistics. It's been proved!"

"I can't help it. Call me a country woman if you must, but I just don't like it."

"Let me speak to Daddy!"

"Your father isn't home, darling."

"Well, when he comes in, you talk to him. Please! Oh, Mother, you can't ruin everything now!"

"Who's ruining what?" asked a voice at the screen door.

Mindy said good-bye to her mother and turned to the front step, where Dana Fraser was standing with a book in his hand. "I heard from Mrs. Moore that you're going to France," he said, as though he had seen her yesterday instead of more than a month ago. "So who's ruining what?"

"My mother!" said Mindy wretchedly. "She doesn't want me to fly."

"That's to be expected," Dana assured her mildly.

"Give her a couple of days to get used to the idea. Generally parents come around." Then he asked, "Aren't you going to invite me in?"

"Excuse me." Mindy unlatched the screen door and held it open.

"I brought you a book about the Louvre."

"The Louvre?"

"It's a museum," Dana teased.

Immediately Mindy was on the defensive. "I know that." She blushed and accepted the book gingerly. "Shall we go out to the terrace or stay in here?"

"The terrace sounds fine," replied Dana. He followed Mindy along the hall and out the back door, then spread himself on a chaise. "Luxury," he commented.

"When do you leave for Paris?" Mindy asked politely. She still held the book, but it was too dark to look at it. "I'm not sure yet. Sometime before the first of the month."

"We're flying over on Labor Day night," Mindy said, suddenly grand.

"Maybe we'll meet. Where are you staying?"

"At a hotel called the Royal Monceau." She gave the information reluctantly, because she wasn't at all sure she wanted Dana Fraser to look her up. Paris might be full of far more fascinating things to do than going to museums with this lanky intellectual. She was sure he'd take her to museums!

However, Dana made no commitments. "The book," he said, "may give you a rough idea of what you'll want to see. Everybody's tastes differ, but you shouldn't miss the Victory of Samothrace and the Mona Lisa. Then you can choose between the classical things and the Impressionists. I just thought the trip might be more fun if you do your homework, so to speak."

"It was very nice of you to think of me." Mindy tried to make her voice polite but icy. After all, he had neglected her for practically the entire summer, so why should she be particularly gracious?

"I want it back," Dana was saying, "but you can keep it a week if you like." He stretched, and asked casually, "What have you been doing with yourself?"

"Working, mostly," Mindy replied honestly instead of yielding to an impulse to say, Oh, having mad fun!

"Me too," said Dana. "I've earned $500 since I saw you last."

"Really?" The sum sounded like a fortune to Mindy.

"I'll need it, in Paris. Are you getting excited about going?"

"Of course. What do you think?"

"I think you *look* excited," Dana said, peering through the dark. "At any rate, you look different from when I saw you last."

"Is that a compliment?"

"It's meant to be. You've lost a good deal of weight."

The same remark from Peter Knox had flattered Mindy, but Dana's reply annoyed her. "You're not very tactful. Suppose I have?"

"It's becoming," Dana said frankly, "but I sort of miss the plump little country cousin. Where has she gone?" He pretended to look under the chaise inquiringly.

"Very funny," muttered Mindy acidly. "Would you like a coke or something?" She felt she had to get up and move around.

"No. No thanks. I really should be going." But Dana made no effort to arise.

Mindy sank back in her chair and looked up at the pale moon sailing high in the sky. "I think you're lucky," she said, "to be going to school in Paris."

Dana nodded in agreement. "I hope my French stands up under the strain."

"I wish I spoke some French," said Mindy wistfully. "Alix says she can manage in hotels and taxis and things, but anything complicated is beyond her. To me, though, she seems to know a lot."

"You'll manage," said Dana confidently. "In restaurants and hotels there's always someone who speaks English. All you really need is to learn how to count in French and understand how much a franc is worth. A new franc, I mean. Sometimes the French quote prices in old francs, which were very different. Hundreds to the dollar, instead of five or so."

"You don't make it sound exactly simple. I hope Alix won't expect me to make change for cash customers," Mindy worried out loud. "Let's see, how does it go? *Un, deux, trois, quatre, cinq, six, sept, neuf, dix. . . .*"

Dana took up the chant. "*Onze, douze, treize, quatorze*, and so on. Then, when you get to seventy, you say *soixante-dix. . . .*"

Mindy listened carefully, but found the explanation hard to follow. "Tell me again," she begged, and this time she nodded with some understanding. "It must help to know as much as you do," she admitted.

"I don't know nearly as much as I should," Dana replied, "but I'm terribly interested, and that's half the battle." He raised his arms and stretched, then pulled at a shaggy forelock. "Guess I'd better be going. Hope you enjoy the book."

During the hurried fortnight that followed, Mindy didn't see Dana Fraser again. He wasn't at home when she returned the book, and although he phoned her later in the evening he merely said good-bye. "I'm leaving tomorrow night," he told her with a surge of boyish enthusiasm in his voice. "And you're off next Monday, aren't you? You'll want a while to get settled, I expect, but I'll try to give you a ring at the Royal Monceau."

"Do try!" Mindy spoke impetuously, because she found her feelings changing. In three short days, with her parents' reluctant permission obtained and passport received, she would be embarking on the same journey. As a stranger in a strange city perhaps, after all, seeing a familiar face might be pleasant.

Business at The Country Cousin was always brisk before a holiday, and there was no time to do more than help the customers. Time raced like a revved-up motor. Paula generously came into the store on Sunday to help Mindy pack the collection of clothes destined for Paris while Alix checked them, item by item, against a typed list. As all three had expected, fitting them into the suitcases was a tight squeeze, and in the end Paula had to sit on top of each one while Alix knelt and fastened the locks.

"There!" she said finally, and sat back on her heels, looking tired and disheveled, but full of pent-up eagerness. "At last," she said, "I believe it. We're really going to get off!"

Mindy's parents drove them to the airport Monday evening. They arrived, as requested by Pan American, a full hour ahead of time. Soon they were joined by Jack and Annette, bearing two white camellias for them to wear on their suits.

So full of suppressed excitement that her mouth was dry and her stomach churning, Mindy nevertheless tried to act grown-up and still her rocketing qualms. Would that huge airplane crouching on the ramp in the dusk really be as safe as people said? Would it shake her to pieces or tip like a boat and make her ill? Her hands were clammy and the weatherbeaten faces of her parents were suddenly very dear.

Then Paula arrived, followed by Irene with Jane and Beth Scott. All of the country cousins were bearing little gifts, small enough to be slipped into a handbag. There were last-minute good wishes, a round of hasty kisses, and suddenly Mindy found herself waving good-bye from the steps of the plane and feeling like a stand-in for a movie star.

The doors were closed and locked, seat belts were fastened, and as the jet taxied over to the runway a stewardess explained the procedure used to inflate a rubber life jacket. This gave Mindy no sense of confidence, but she couldn't admit her fears to Alix, who looked utterly relaxed and delighted to be off. Instead she sat rigid, every muscle tensed, as the plane sailed smoothly up into the air.

After several moments she turned to Alix in unconcealed surprise. "Is that all there is to it?" she asked.

Twelve

The night was short. Dinner was served as soon as the jet reached cruising altitude, and the meal was followed by a motion picture for which Mindy and Alix plugged in earphones. By the time the movie was over they were both uncontrollably sleepy, so a stewardess brought them small pillows and blankets. They kicked off their shoes and lay back, dozing until streamers of dawn pierced the dark sky. Then, along with the rest of the passengers, they roused to sip orange juice and coffee, but sternly bypassed the sweet rolls.

"We won't be able to resist the *croissants* in Paris," Alix predicted, "so from anything that isn't pluperfect I shall abstain."

Mindy followed suit. She liked being slim and wanted to remain so. Besides, she was still too keyed up to be really hungry, and the day breaking with such brilliance in the east was bound to be one she would never forget. Who needed a sticky bun?

As the sun rose in the sky the jet descended through whipped-cream clouds, circling to the north while the pilot waited for clearance at Orly. Suddenly Mindy clutched her cousin's wrist. "There it is!" she cried, tears starting to her eyes and spilling over.

"There what is?" Alix leaned forward, trying to see.

"The Eiffel Tower, looking just like the Eiffel Tower! My goodness but I'm glad I read all those books!" Mindy got out a handkerchief and blew her nose. "Do you think I'm silly?"

"Not in the least." Alix patted Mindy's hand. "I'd be disappointed if you weren't terribly excited. After all, think of the fun for me, to see it all again through fresh eyes!" She gathered up her handbag and began to put on her gloves, the businesswoman once more. "Let's hope we get through customs without too much delay."

This, however, was not to be the case. Having explained, haltingly, that the two heavy suitcases contained commercial samples, Alix and Mindy were ushered to an office at the end of the building, where two men took the cases to a large closet containing a great deal of other luggage, put them inside, and locked the door.

"Oh, no!" Alix cried. "I must take those with me."

"*Mais, madame*," protested the inspector, who was assisting the American lady, "*ce n'est pas possible.*" Then in voluble French he tried to give the reasons.

Mindy, standing by, heard one recurring word: *transitaire*. "He's saying we can't pay the bond directly. We've got to have a middleman," Alix explained after nearly half an hour wasted in an attempt to communicate. "That much I can understand."

"*C'est nécessaire!*" the Frenchman said, nodding happily. "*Un transitaire.*" To Mindy the words sounded like a nonsense rhyme, and she had to stifle a wild desire to giggle.

But to Mrs. Moore it was no laughing matter. "*Quelle horreur!*" she cried, in real distress. "But no one told us! How is this possible?"

Again there was a spate of conversation between the two, although Mindy suspected that neither had more than an occasional clue concerning what the other was saying. Finally, however, after crossing the room and rummaging through a file for about ten minutes, the inspector came back with a typed list and handed it to Alix with a beaming smile.

"*Les transitaires!*" he shouted. "*Ici.*"

"*Ici* where?" asked Alix, as Mindy looked over her shoulder at a list of names. "*Où sont les transitaires?*"

This question entailed another consultation, from which one new fact emerged. There were many *transitaires* to be found in the freight building, which, unfortunately, was some distance away. No, there was no way for the inspector to transport the American ladies hence. Yes, it was possible to walk, but it was very far. Orly was a large airport. A taxi would be desirable, although a taxi driver might be reluctant to take passengers for such a short ride.

"All right. Let's go," said Alix, turning once more to Mindy. "*Merci, monsieur.*" She smiled sweetly and pointed toward the locked closet. "*Nous reviendrons.*"

"*À votre service,*" murmured the inspector, bowing from the waist. For a moment Mindy thought he might even kiss Alix's hand, not in courtesy so much as in relief, but instead he moved away and put fingers to his forehead as though he had barely survived a traumatic experience.

Back past the customs officials Mindy followed her cousin, and once more a good deal of red tape had to be cut. Their personal luggage must be checked and permission obtained to re-enter the building and return to the inspector's office. Everything took time.

But finally they arrived at the freight office with a driver who kept muttering inprecations. Even Mindy could tell that they were imprecations, although she understood barely a dozen words of French. Alix refused to be concerned, however. She tipped the man liberally for his trouble and walked briskly into the first office she could find that had the word *Transitaire* on the door.

The man behind a desk in the center of the room

looked surprised to see two young women, and Americans to boot. Alix again used her halting French to explain that she needed a customs broker, and the man nodded and seemed pleased, but he glanced anxiously at his watch, which made Mindy look at hers. It was exactly twelve o'clock.

"*C'est l'heure du déjeuner*," the *transitaire* explained. Alix shut her eyes and groaned, because she knew what was coming. "Come back at two o'clock," he advised her. "We will then discuss the matter of business, *oui?*"

"*Oui*," Alix agreed reluctantly. "Come along, Mindy. We'll walk, this time, since we know the way. Fortunately, in France even an airport lunch counter can produce a very respectable meal."

To Mindy the lunch seemed more than respectable. The beef stew was delicious, the salad greens crisp, and the crusty bread more flavorful than any she had ever tasted. Mopping up the last of her sauce, she sighed happily. "I see what you mean about French cooking. Is it all going to be as good as this?"

"Better," Alix promised, and turned to glance at a clock on the wall behind them. "Another hour to go. Well, we can wander through the airport and look around. People watching is always fun in France."

The hour passed, slowly but not unpleasantly, and again they went back to the freight office, where the *transitaire* explained that forms must be filled out and a bond posted. The procedure was all very complex and would take much time. "Come back tomorrow," he advised.

Alix shook her head firmly, and insisted, "Today."

The man behind the desk shrugged and spread his hands. "*Ce n'est pas possible.*" He led Alix to the door and pointed down the hall, advising her in a flood of French to try someone else.

Again Mindy tagged along at her cousin's heels, at length finding herself in a shabby, dirty little office with two dubious-looking characters whom Alix later described as looking like refugees from the Place Pigalle. Once more the problem was outlined, and these men seemed to understand.

"Why, certainly. *Revenez demain,*" they advised in unison. Come back tomorrow.

Alix kept her temper, but again shook her head, and Mindy gathered she was explaining that a nice man down the hall would take care of the matter tomorrow. If they wanted the business they must act today. This demand apparently was quite revolutionary, but the idea seemed to penetrate that there was profit today, no profit tomorrow. At this point they asked *madame* and *mademoiselle* to be seated, and one of the men picked up a telephone.

"What is he saying?" Mindy whispered, after Alix assured her that he had capitulated and was calling a colleague concerning their problem.

The stream of impassioned French pouring forth was

beyond even Alix's comprehension. "I haven't the slightest notion," she admitted, "but at least he seems to be trying to get somewhere, which is more than anyone else has done."

"Suppose we *have* to come back tomorrow?" Mindy asked in an undertone.

"We can't. The Country Cousin opens for business at nine thirty." Alix thrust out her chin pugnaciously, but settled back into a ladylike attitude when the man, having finished talking, nodded encouragingly and asked to see her list of merchandise.

There came a long period of laborious questions and answers. Then the two men began to type out forms and total Alix's price list on an antique adding machine. Mindy became so sleepy she kept yawning behind her hand. Would this process never end?

An hour passed, then half of another, but finally, accompanied by both men, Mindy and Alix were whisked back to the main building in a tiny car and led once more into the inspector's office. Now, it seemed, they were all friends. There was much handshaking and joking in which Alix, smiling happily, seemed to share.

Mindy marveled at her cousin's patience, because she must be exhausted, but apparently trying to hurry proceedings at this point was useless. Once the amenities were over a key was produced and the door to the fateful closet finally opened. "Will *madame* please identify her luggage?" the inspector asked.

Gladly! Alix walked across the room prepared to point to the two suitcases, then turned to Mindy with a stricken expression. "Our luggage isn't here!"

"It must be!" Mindy hurried to the closet and peered inside anxiously.

"*Les valises ne sont pas ici,*" Alix repeated to the inspector, who threw up his hands in despair.

"They must be!" he insisted, just as Mindy had a moment before.

All semblance of camaraderie fled. Everyone began to shout at one another in indistinguishable French, everyone prodded and pulled at the bags and parcels in the closet, and in turn everyone began to consult the time.

"I know the next bit by heart," Alix muttered to Mindy. " '*Revenez demain.*' If I hear those words once more I'm going to scream."

She didn't scream, but when the inspector said, "*Madame, je regrette mais il faut revenir demain,*" she did something quite untypical. She sank down in the nearest chair, pulled a handkerchief from her purse, and burst into tears.

This reaction, instead of eliciting compassion, made the Frenchmen even more anxious to put everything off until the next morning. "But I can't come back tomorrow," Alix cried. "*C'est impossible!*" It will be disastrous, the failure of all my months of planning."

Sadly, the inspector and the *transitaires* shook their

heads. Obviously they couldn't understand what all the rush was about. The pretty American lady was unduly upset.

"What are we going to do?" By this time even Mindy was wringing her hands.

"I don't know," replied Alix dully. Since tears had been useless, she dried her eyes, stood up, and said, "If only I spoke better French. If only I could make them understand!"

"Maybe I can help you," suggested a familiar American voice from the door, and together Mindy and Alix whirled around. Dana Fraser was standing there as casually as though he had just arrived at Mrs. Moore's house in Saint Davids. His hair was shaggy and wind-tossed as usual, and his trousers needed a press. Instead of a jacket he was wearing a sweater that had seen better days, but to Mindy and Alix he was a knight in shining armor, a knight who could speak really adequate French!

"Dana! Oh, my dear boy, you're an absolute godsend. Try to make these men understand that we open up shop tomorrow morning and that we've simply got to get our samples out of hock tonight. They keep insisting we must come back tomorrow, but such a delay will ruin everything. After all, I've sent out notices to a mailing list of three hundred people and I've advertised the opening date in the *Paris Tribune*."

Dana nodded, accepting the situation without question. He spoke rapidly but politely in French to the inspector, who kept nodding with dawning understanding. After some time he stepped forward, shook Dana's hand, and beckoned to the *transitaires*. Within a few moments all three walked through the office door and disappeared.

"Where are they going?" asked Alix.

"To try to find the suitcases."

Mindy, unable to stifle her curiosity a moment longer, asked, "What are *you* doing here, Dana?"

"Trying to find a lost suitcase—what else? Only half my baggage arrived with me, and you know the French. *"Revenez demain."*

"Revenez demain," parroted Mindy. "Those are two words I'll never forget."

"Well, that's one way of learning a language," Dana teased. "It's slow, but it's—"

"Oh, look! Dana, Mindy—" Alix pointed to the window, through which could be seen the inspector, marching ahead of the two *transitaires*, who were triumphantly lugging two heavy suitcases across the tarmac. "Dana, how can I thank you? Have dinner with us to celebrate, tomorrow night! Can you do that?"

"It would be great, if my own luggage turns up by then. I haven't even got a clean shirt."

"Voilà!" As proud as though he had won a major

battle, the inspector at that moment led his winded troops into the office. "*Voilà, madame!*"

The suitcases were opened and the samples checked, while Dana at last was able to tackle the subject of his own missing luggage with the inspector.

Meanwhile, Alix concluded her business with the *transitaires*. She presented them with unsigned travelers' checks as bond, paid them their commission in French francs, and gave each a *pourboire* for his extra trouble in accomplishing everything that afternoon.

Dana and the inspector had both disappeared into the mysterious closet, from which there soon came a typically American whoop of delight. Dana emerged, more disheveled than ever, bearing a shabby traveling bag. "Here it is!" he announced happily. "Boy, am I in luck!"

Alix heaved a grateful sigh. "At last we're free!" She turned to Dana. "Please, share our taxi, at least as far as the Étoile."

During the ride which followed everyone, weak with relief, laughed uproariously at everything and nothing. Mindy was conscious of a divided highway leading through countryside that gradually changed to high-rise suburban developments and finally to the gray and mauve streets of the city. Everything shouted Paris: the orange awnings of the cafés, the flower sellers, the string bags on women's arms, the cobblestones and the wispy trees, the straight façades of the close-packed buildings. She clasped her hands and fell silent as the taxi sped along the river, then turned and ducked into a maze of streets that led to the hotel.

For her, the sequence of events now became confused. A doorman opened the taxi door, a porter came for the luggage, she gathered up magazines and hand baggage, and somewhere along the line Dana disappeared, to the accompaniment of repeated thanks and the promise that he would come to the hotel at eight the following night.

By this time Mindy was asleep standing up, but at the sight of the elegant French salon into which they were ushered by the bellboy she revived enough to murmur, "How simply darling!" Then she went through to the bedroom Alix and she were to share and walked like a somnambulist to the nearest bed.

An hour's nap revived her remarkably, and after awakening she was once more eager for adventure. When Alix proposed that they take a walk after unpacking the samples, she agreed enthusiastically. "Oh, let's hurry, please!"

Again the suitcases were opened, and Mindy shook out evening frocks, taffeta raincoats, woolen and silk dresses, slacks and skirts, while Alix rang for a chambermaid and requested more hangers.

The woman looked at the collection of clothes in

astonishment, apparently accustomed to Americans with large wardrobes but never with such a plethora of costumes. To make her understand that these clothes were for sale took a little time, but when comprehension dawned she brought armloads of hangers quite willingly. The American ladies weren't rich tourists, after all, but simple working women like herself, and from then on nothing was too much trouble. She even produced two old-fashioned wooden clotheshorses, which she called by a French name that sounded like "parrots." They accommodated sweaters and skirts and blouses very nicely, leaving the long closet in the salon's entrance hall free for the more important clothes.

The minute everything was unpacked, Alix cried, "Come, Mindy, let's get out of here. We don't want to miss the twilight."

Like a pair of children excused from school, they picked up their gloves and purses and almost ran from the hotel toward the Arc de Triomphe, which loomed in the circle called l'Étoile at the end of the street. The avenue Hoche, like eleven others, formed spokes of a wheel converging on the famous monument to Napoleon's conquests, beneath which lies the grave of an unknown World War I soldier for whom a flame continually burns.

Around the great arch traffic swirled with such abandon that even Alix hesitated to cross. "The *circulation,* as the French say, is certainly intense."

"I'll say it is," Mindy was agreeing when a fat man in a beret, followed by his wife and four small children waddling like a family of ducks, plunged past them into the melee. He halted all cars by extending a broad palm, so Alix grabbed Mindy's hand and hurried in his wake. They reached the safety of the Étoile without mishap, and, still unconsciously holding hands, turned to look down the length of the wide and busy avenue leading straight as a die to the Place de la Concorde far in the distance.

"We can take a bus," Alix was saying, "and ride as far as Notre Dame, then cross over to the Left Bank, and have dinner at a little restaurant I know."

"That would be lovely," Mindy breathed, thinking that anything would be lovely, that just being there was lovely enough.

Then, at that precise moment, as if a current were raised on a stage and the play was about to begin, every light along the Champs Élysées flashed on. All the stars in the skies seemed to have converged on Paris. The scene was fairyland!

Thirteen

Before she opened her eyes the next morning two images floated in Mindy's consciousness. One was a vision of the glittering Champs Élysées, and the other was the sight of Dana's face when he had emerged from the closet at the airport triumphantly bearing the recovered traveling bag.

Then, remembering that she was in Paris, Mindy sat up with a start. Her cousin's bed was empty, and there was the sound of water running in the *salle de bain*. The figured linen curtains, drawn the night before, had been pulled back to let in the wan morning light.

Mindy clasped her knees in her arms and looked around ecstatically at the paneled walls painted robin's-egg blue, at the *escritoire* and the Louis Quinze chest and the curved night tables. Her bright yellow down puff, too short to be of much use, had fallen to the floor, but her dressing gown lay at the foot of the bed.

She pulled it around her shoulders and went over to the long French windows. Beyond them was a grilled iron railing, and by leaning far out she could see the Arc de Triomphe looming in the distance. Yes, it was all true. She was staying in a beautiful suite in the Royal Monceau, she had dined last night on *blanquette de veau* in a restaurant overlooking the Seine, and for two long and lovely weeks she would be able to drink up the enchanting atmosphere of Paris.

There was a knock at the salon door, and she opened it to a waiter wheeling a round table dressed with a cloth of spanking white linen and laid with places for two. Alix emerged from the bathroom at the sound of the muted clatter of china, and they pulled up chairs and breakfasted on *café au lait* and warm, flaky *croissants*.

Alix didn't linger over the meal. She finished dressing quickly and rang for the obliging chambermaid, explaining that everything must be made ready *"pour les clientes."* In the salon she arranged two rather touching appurtenances of The Country Cousin, a guest book bound in bright linen and a cookie jar filled with macaroons made by Mindy's mother. In Bryn Mawr the cookie jar was as familiar as the view from the window, but in the hotel it looked defenseless and oddly out of place.

They lay on a round table, topped with brown marble, which in turn stood on an Oriental throw rug placed precisely in the center of the red-carpeted reception room. Nearby stood a pair of gray-painted carved French chairs upholstered in brown plush. "The plush reminds me of my grandmother," Alix said, as she ran a hand over it. Two gilt-framed pier glasses flanked one another on opposite walls above half-round marble-topped tables. There were ponderous standing lamps, inlaid chests, and cherry-red damask curtains that set off gray-green walls.

In the days to follow Mindy was to know each piece of furniture intimately, but on this first morning everything seemed fascinatingly different. She ran her fingers over the long pierced brass panels that backed the door handles and exclaimed about the crystal chandeliers, but Alix seemed engrossed with business detail. She stacked sales pads, rearranged dresses on the racks, sorted sweaters, and made the chic little salon look more and more like a shop.

Meanwhile, maids vacuumed the rugs, dusted furniture, and made beds. By nine o'clock everything was immaculate, but Alix was growing increasingly tense. "Suppose nobody comes?" she asked, as she paced up and down the room.

"Well, anyway," she replied, answering her own question, "it's nice to be in Paris, and a few people will certainly see our ad in the paper, even though it isn't in a very good location, right next to Alcoholics Anonymous."

Mindy tried to laugh, but she wasn't really amused by the remark and her lips felt stiff. She knew how apprehensive Alix must be. They were in Paris, the fashion capital of the world, and The Country Cousin in Bryn Mawr was far away. Cold terror began to seep through Mindy's veins. She perched on the edge of a chair, and croaked, "Don't worry, Alix. At least not yet."

"Oh, I won't!" With false bravado Alix rearranged a pile of Villager blouses for the third time. "We didn't really expect to sell too much, and, after all, the trip will be marvelous."

Nine-thirty came and went. "I should have bought some flowers," Alix said. "I'll do that this afternoon."

Mindy tried to be brave and hopeful. "Maybe the first day will be like a Monday in Bryn Mawr," she said. "Mondays are always slow."

At ten o'clock, while Alix was nervously applying fresh lipstick in the bedroom, the telephone in the salon rang and Mindy leaped to answer it. The voice of the concierge, who spoke excellent English, came over the wire. "Mrs. Money is in the lobby," he announced. "Is it all right for her to come up?"

"Of course," Mindy managed to say before laughter overcame her. She let the receiver fall with a clatter, and gasped between giggles, "Mrs. Money is downstairs, believe it or not. She's coming right up!"

The phone rang again, and this time Alix answered. "Yes, our clothes are priced from twenty dollars to seventy dollars," she replied in careful French.

Mindy, standing by, could hear the squeal at the other end of the wire. "*Mon Dieu!*"

She'll be right over, Alix said with amused relief to Mindy as Mrs. Money—she must be Mrs. Money!— appeared in the open hall door.

Following her was a dumpy American woman with two gangly daughters in tow. Mindy, slipping past Alix and the first client, greeted the trio cheerfully. Maybe everything would be all right after all.

The woman introduced herself. "I'm Mrs. Murdock from Doylestown, P.A. My brother owns the Fairtrade Food Market in Wayne," she said.

"Why, Mrs. Murdock, how nice to see you," said Mindy cordially. "Do you live in Paris?"

"Temporarily," Mrs. Murdock replied without enthusiasm. "The girls want tweed skirts and Shetland sweaters for school."

"Of course. Here are the samples. There isn't every color in every size, but you can make your selections and we'll be glad to send anything you decide upon."

While the girls and their mother hovered around the "*parrot*" hung with skirts, blouses, and sweaters, Alix discovered that Mrs. Money was actually Madame Manet, a journalist who wrote a column for the *Washington Star*.

"I'd like to do a story about you," she said to Alix. "Bringing The Country Cousin to Paris is very exciting. But first I want to buy some of these wonderful American clothes."

After making several selections from the samples hung in the hall closets *madame*-the-reporter followed Alix into the bedroom to try them on. "The interview can wait," Mindy heard the Frenchwoman say in charmingly accented English. "Oh, this is very chic. I must have it. In black, that's the most distinguished. And this one is ravishing. I think in green, don't you? The marvelous thing is, if you buy something inexpensive in Paris everybody knows where it comes from, but if you get a dress like this from the United States nobody has seen it and it could be any price."

Fifteen minutes later the woman who had squealed "*mon Dieu*" over the phone arrived with a friend. Both were so tall and elegant that Mindy wasn't surprised to learn that they had been fashion models. While Alix exclaimed over the Chanel suit one of them was wearing they exclaimed over the collection, and within minutes they had stripped to demibras and bikini panties, one set in black and the other in brown, and were excitedly trying on clothes.

Mrs. Murdock and her daughters, who were seated on the sofa ostensibly inspecting a folder of John Meyer sweater colors, could scarcely keep their eyes from the open bedroom door. Three gaping mouths testified to their astonishment, which Mindy shared. Compared to such scanty French underwear, the Murdock girls' American white nylon slips seemed tame indeed!

From that time on the salon was never empty. Customers came and went, sales slips were written and postage figured, depending upon whether the *cliente* wished her purchases shipped by air, surface, or Army Post Office. Not until nearly two o'clock did Alix have time to order lunch. When a waiter finally wheeled a table into the bedroom Mindy was starved, and the omelet and salad and French rolls tasted like ambrosia. The afternoon was almost as busy as the morning, and at five thirty Alix closed the double doors leading to the hall thankfully. "Whew!" she breathed. "Just for fun, let's figure up the D.B."

Usually totaling the sales slips that had accumulated on the spike at The Country Cousin was no great chore. In Paris, however, there were checks in francs as well as in dollars and some cash as well. Mindy's tentative arithmetic was unequal to the task, but finally a tally was arrived at, and the sum was sufficiently substantial to make Alix whistle cheerfully.

"Well, we'll have naps and baths and then we'll take

Dana out and buy him a good dinner. Now it's really time to celebrate!"

Paris at night was a joy to behold. In a small taxi, with Alix and Mindy in back and Dana jackknifed into the front seat beside the driver, they sped down the faubourg Saint Honoré and the rue Saint Honoré to Les Halles, the old market district where one of Alix's favorite restaurants was located. The name was a famous one, but the inside, on first inspection, disappointed Mindy. It looked dark and Victorian, and the black-coated, white-aproned waiters might have stepped from a Toulouse-Lautrec drawing instead of the kitchen of a contemporary restaurant.

The food, however, was Lucullan. Alix, at her own suggestion, ordered for all three, and they had artichoke hearts, sole Maison with a superb sauce, salad, and soufflé Grand Marnier. By ten they were finished. Alix paid the waiter, and said, "Dana, I'm going back to the hotel and rest up for tomorrow, but Mindy's young and it's her first trip abroad. Give her a glimpse of Paris at night."

For Mindy to protest was useless. In a trice her cousin was in a cab headed uptown, while she and Dana were left on the corner by the restaurant, surrounded by crates of amethyst grapes and yellow apples and all sorts of produce from the French countryside.

"This is a sight in itself," said Dana. The wholesale

markets were not yet open but great trucks lined the streets and burly young men handed down box after box of vegetables and fruit to be stacked on the sidewalks.

There were pomegranates from Morocco and carrots from Crécy-sur-Morin. There were small polished potatoes and black earth-coated truffles that had recently been rooted out by young sows in Périgord. There were hothouse raspberries and late strawberries and open boxes of the biggest grapes Mindy had ever seen, of a curious translucent yellow so tempting that she suddenly put out her hand, seized one, and popped it into her mouth.

A mustached man in shirt sleeves approaching along the dimly lighted street broke into a run. "*Non, non, non!*" he cried, shaking a finger in the air.

Guiltily, Mindy destroyed the evidence by swallowing the grape. She envisioned herself being hauled to the prefecture of police and spending the night in a Paris jail. Cringing against Dana, she tried to frame a French apology. "*Je regrette—*" Then she broke off and wailed, "They just looked so good!"

The man had gone to the open box, from which he turned toward her, holding a heavy bunch of the luscious grapes in his fingers. Heels together, he bowed with a special flourish. "*Pour mademoiselle, avec mes compliments,*" he said with all the elegance of an aristocrat.

Mindy was so surprised that she stammered her thanks. "*Merci, monsieur. Pour moi?* But it's too much!"

Dana, standing by, was enjoying her confusion. He said something in French to the merchant at which they both laughed, then shook hands in amicable parting, while Mindy pulled grapes off the stem one by one and murmured "Mmm" as she tasted them. A few moments later Dana was sharing her unexpected gift, and before they emerged from the winding streets of Les Halles to a broad boulevard the grapes were gone.

Without asking her what she'd like to do or telling her where they were going, Dana hailed a cab, which hurtled through the dark streets and began to climb a hill bright with cafés hung with awnings and neon lights. "This is the section called Montmartre," he said after a while. "The basilica of Sacré Coeur stands on the very top—the *butte*, the French call it—and from the steps we'll be able to see the lights of Paris spread out for miles around."

The taxi dropped them off at the Place du Tertre, a square filled with trees and small tables at which only a few people sat on this early fall evening, because there was a definite chill in the air. But Mindy wasn't cold. She was warmed by the good food and the glass of muscadet she had drunk at dinner. She felt like skipping and running; to be alive was wonderful.

Dana seemed to share her mood. He took her hand

and hurried her through narrow alleys that led up and up again until the basilica emerged, white and moon-struck, directly above them. Then they climbed the steps breathlessly to reach the view from the parapet.

Other young couples were there, leaning close and whispering together as they looked down on the carpet of twinkling lights. Dana tucked Mindy's arm through his with an authority she found rather pleasant. "There it is, little girl," he said. "Think of the men who have stood on this hill with Paris spread below them, the artists who have painted and the kings who have ruled and the writers who have yearned over this beautiful city. Think of the wars and the revolutions she has seen—Napoleon's conquering armies and the tumbril carrying Marie Antoinette to the guillotine. It's a miracle that Paris could survive everything—even the last two wars."

Chills traced their way down Mindy's spine. "It's something pretty special, all right," she said, wishing she had Dana's knack for putting feelings into words. "It must be marvelous to know you're going to be in Paris all winter and can come up here any time you like."

"Whoa! I'm going to be working," Dana reminded her.

"Studying, you mean."

"And you don't call studying work?"

They turned and started back down the hill, chatting

companionably. Mindy realized that she no longer felt that Dana was odd or different, because in Paris there were no smooth young men like Peter Knox with whom to compare him. He looked like any one of a dozen young American students she had seen walking the streets or poring over bargains in the bookstalls along the Seine. And she was genuinely glad to be with him. Without Dana she might have looked down on Paris from the *butte* without really seeing it at all.

"There's a little cabaret I've been to just once," he was saying now. "It's called the Lapin Agile. Let's see if we can find it, unless you're too tired."

"I'm not tired at all," Mindy said, and meant it. A cabaret sounded slightly wicked, but since she was sure Dana wouldn't take her anywhere disreputable she went along with him willingly.

"This is a place Utrillo and a good many other Impressionists painted," Dana said, as they approached a single-storied, smoke-blackened building on the corner of a narrow cobbled street. "It has a romantic history. Originally it was supposed to have been the hunting lodge of Henry the Fourth, but later it was the home of a political cartoonist named André Gill, who painted a rabbit above the door, then blew his brains out in the kitchen. Le Lapin à Gill became Le Lapin Agile—the Agile Rabbit. It's really a pun, you see."

He opened the door to a small bar, which apparently served as a waiting room, because from behind a curtained doorway came the sound of a guitar and a male voice raised in song.

"*C'est l'amour, c'est sa flamme. . . .*"

"How I wish I'd studied French in high school!" whispered Mindy passionately.

"It's not too late," Dana whispered back, "and now you have a reason."

"A reason?"

"You will come to Paris again, won't you?"

"I hope so, but how can I be sure?"

"Because you'll want to. You'll want to very much. Mindy, you're just awakening. You're like Sleeping Beauty, and maybe Paris will be—" Dana broke off as the curtain was pulled aside, and they were swept into the main room on a tide of new arrivals. Long tavern tables and benches were crowded into every foot of space and occupied by all kinds of people, young and old, shabby and well-dressed, French and foreign. Seated halfway up a flight of steps in the corner, a young man strummed a guitar lazily and adjusted the strings. Then, as the door closed once more, he began to sing.

"*Filles, chantez le mois de mai. . . .*"

Mindy understood not a word, but the music was haunting and beautiful. She sat as rapt as the rest of the audience until finally Dana said, "At the next break I'll have to take you home. It's nearly one o'clock."

Fourteen

The next day Caroline Paige and a bevy of twittering *lycée* classmates sailed into the suite at the Royal Monceau in a flying wedge. The French girls settled on the John Meyer sweaters and skirts like chickadees on sunflower seeds, and while Mindy wrote up the sales slips for their purchases, Caroline said, "Mummy wants to have a little supper party for you, Mrs. Moore. She's going to phone you late this afternoon and set a date."

This invitation was the first of several, and Mindy was included in many of them. Alix had made a number of French acquaintances on her previous trip, and she also knew a few Americans living in Paris. "We'd better start a social calendar," she suggested gaily to Mindy. "We're getting popular."

This was quite true. The United Press sent a photographer and a reporter to the hotel to prepare a release for United States newspapers on the venture. French retailers and manufacturers came in to look over the collection. Mrs. Moore's acquaintances called or dropped by and bought clothes. Business was delightfully brisk.

Because there was no way to find time for a proper lunch, the cousins took to picnicking on soft drinks and *sandwiches de jambon et fromage*, which could be picked up at a corner café and brought back to the hotel. The first day Mindy was sent on this errand the French words fled her memory at the very minute she approached the counter. "Two ham and cheese sandwiches," she stammered, and pointed to long thin arrangements of French bread that looked more like American submarines than anything else.

The Paige supper party was set for Sunday night, as a climax to a free day which Mindy anticipated happily. Alix had arranged to rent a small car and invited Dana to join them on an expedition to Versailles.

It was a flawless September morning, mild and beckoning. The leaves in the trees rustled with a presage of fall, but the air was soft and a shy Parisian sun hovered overhead. "The interesting thing about the Paris sky is that it's so high," Mindy commented, as they drove along an avenue skirting the Bois. "Why is that, I wonder?"

Neither Alix nor Dana had an answer, but the question engendered a discussion about the character of the light in Paris. For centuries that peculiar, indescribable luminescence, which Mindy sensed when she spoke of the height of the sky, had been attracting artists to the city. After a while she clapped her hands in sheer exuberance, and cried, "Imagine, just being here!"

"And imagine going to Versailles on such a perfect day," caroled Alix.

"I've always been there in the rain before," said Dana. "On a morning like this the park should be marvelous."

The park was marvelous indeed, a bright tapestry of carefully planned color set off by borders of green grass, with fountains playing and beyond the *tapis vert* the water of the Grand Canal glistening in the distance. But the magnificent palace itself intrigued Mindy especially. She stood entranced in the huge Hall of Mirrors and walked rapturously through the redecorated reception rooms of Louis Fourteenth's royal suite. The picture gallery also interested her, particularly the great David paintings, filled with kings and courtiers wearing costumes so heavy with gold embroidery she could almost feel their weight on her own back.

"Just look!" she cried. "Just look at these clothes. Aren't the velvets and satins something you want to touch?"

"Clothes again," Dana chided her. "Can't you ever get your mind off clothes?"

"But I love them," Mindy countered. "I get a thrill

—an actual thrill—out of fabrics. The cat's-tongue scratchiness of a good tweed, the buttery hand of a certain sort of silk, the heavy slipperiness of satin. You're fascinated by Oriental languages, Dana. Why shouldn't I be fascinated by fabrics and clothes?"

She spoke, as she had spoken to Peter Knox on the Fourth of July at the farm, straight from the heart. She wasn't thinking about making an impression or about how her feelings would be received, and as a consequence Dana stopped and listened. "You could be right," he said. "It doesn't matter much what you're committed to, so long as you're thoroughly committed."

Mindy smiled. "You know, my sister-in-law said the same thing, in a slightly different way." For the first time she had admitted Annette as a member of the family. Once more she had spoken unselfconsciously, and she was aware that a hurdle had been crossed. Far from home on the other side of the Atlantic she had capitulated at last. No longer was she treating Annette as an outsider, but as a relative.

"Come along, you two," Alix urged, as she crossed the gallery to join them. "It's time to get outdoors again. I want to sit at a sidewalk table in the sun and have an omelet and a salad and some *vin de pays*."

After lunch the trio went to visit the Petite Trianon, where Marie Antoinette had played at being a milkmaid. Then they returned to the palace and were led through the royal family apartments available to visitors only on guided tours. As the afternoon drew to a close Mindy felt positively surfeited with sights to remember. "A customer said yesterday, after I'd showed her a number of dresses, 'Don't tell me so much at one time; I can't absorb it.' Now I know just how she felt."

"A little knowledge is a dangerous thing," Dana warned her. "When you go home you'll want to read all about the history of Versailles and the French Revolution."

"You're so right!" Mindy agreed. "Oh, what a lot there is to learn!"

Such enthusiasm seemed to please Dana, because he grinned companionably, and said to Alix, "Its fun to shepherd this little lamb, isn't it?"

"Don't be supercilious," Mindy retorted. "Next time I come to Paris I'm going to know a thing or two."

"And I'll wager she does," Alix chimed in. "All Mindy needed was to have her curiosity aroused."

The statement wasn't entirely true. Mindy knew that she needed other things as well: poise, self-confidence, more education. But what a lot she had learned in this one short summer. How far she had come from the green-stone farmhouse in the Oley Valley to the marble halls of Versailles.

And Paris! Just to walk down the avenue Hoche to

the café on the corner in quest of a *sandwich de jambon* was pure joy. To stroll in the Parc Monceau among the flowers planted beneath the crumbling colonnade was to be transported back in time to the turn of the century. To pass the flower market at the Madeleine was to store away a bright painting she would own forever. To travel half a mile by taxi was like a breathtaking ride on a scenic railway. And to eat in a French restaurant, be it grand or ever so humble, was to experience a taste sensation she would never forget.

"Dreaming, darling?" Alix touched her arm.

Mindy nodded. Dreaming with her eyes wide open, but she was powerless to put her sensations into words.

Back at the hotel the cousins bathed and changed while Dana waited in the salon, reading a paperback he had pulled from the pocket of his tweed jacket. Ready before Alix, Mindy joined him and looked him over critically. "Shouldn't you have gone back to your room and put on something more—well, more . . . ?"

Dana glanced up with a hurt expression, then stood and jerked at the jacket, finally bending to look down at his unpressed pants. "I like this suit." He sounded both indignant and offended. "It makes me feel like Dylan Thomas. What's the matter with it, anyway?"

Mindy sighed. "It doesn't look exactly right for a dinner party."

"This is Sunday night supper. Very casual. Like me."

Mindy's mouth twitched in amusement. Reprimanding Dana and making it stick was impossible. He sat down again and arranged his long legs gracefully over an arm of the plush chair. "Besides, it's half an hour by Metro to where I live."

Mindy changed the subject. "What are you reading?"

"A novel by Camus."

"In French?"

Dana nodded. "You always lose something in translation, I think."

Mindy perched on the edge of the sofa, being careful not to wrinkle her skirt. "I wish I could read French. Both you and Alix make me feel I've wasted so much time!"

"Suppose you have? You're still young. You can learn a lot in a couple of years."

"And I'm going to," Mindy promised. "When you see me again I'll be able to conjugate French verbs and —and everything."

"When I see you again. You mean this coming week?"

"No, silly. I mean next year."

"Oh, so I'm to see you next year, but not next week?"

Inevitably, when she was teased, Mindy flushed. She glanced down at the toes of her slippers and wished she had a knack for repartee.

Dana rescued her. "My classes don't begin for a while

yet. I thought we might go to see Sainte Chapelle together and maybe go out on the river sometime in a *bateau mouche*."

"A what?"

"A *bateau mouche*, a fly boat. It's an apt name, because the boats are flat-bottomed, and they skitter over the Seine like dragonflies. You must have seen them, tied up near the Place d'Alma or the Pont Neuf."

Since these spots were outside her Parisian frame of reference, Mindy shook her head. "Remember, I have to work until five thirty every day," she warned.

"*Every* day?"

"Of course."

"I'll talk to Mrs. Moore. I bet she'll let you off some afternoon," Dana suggested in a conspiratorial whisper.

"You will not talk to her," Mindy flared. "This is my job, and you won't ask favors of my boss!"

Dana put up his hands defensively and pretended to shrink back. "Whoa there! Calm down. It was just an idea."

"A bad one. If you think I'm going to run out on my cousin after she's brought me along on this wonderful trip!"

"Forget it. I'm duly reprimanded. Anyway, the river boats run in the evenings, and we may still have some warmish nights."

Alix came into the room ready to leave, with a light coat over one arm. "Am I interrupting an argument?"

Dana got to his feet. "Almost, but you were a minute too late. I capitulated."

Alix raised her eyebrows. "Hear, hear!" Then she glanced at the wall clock. "I think we'd better hurry."

The Paiges' apartment in Neuilly was high up in a modern building with huge glass windows looking out over the streaming city traffic. Street lamps glowed dimly, outclassed by neon advertising signs, and far in the distance the cone of the Eiffel Tower was outlined in electric lights.

Mindy could scarcely tear her eyes away from the view, which Mr. Paige showed her with all the pride of possession that a boy might have over his first bicycle. "My womenfolk would be glad to go back to the States tomorrow," he confessed in an undertone. "But I love it here."

"Now, Daddy!" Caroline came up, waggling a finger. "You mustn't let him start his sales pitch about Paris, Mindy. He can go on for hours."

"So could I, if I could find the words." Mindy smiled up at the tall, gray-haired man understandingly, but allowed herself to be carried off by Caroline, who wanted to show her the rest of the apartment. "It's sort of crazy. Even in a new building like this one the *salle de bain* and the *cabinet de toilette* are separate, so that you get tangled up in all the doors. And here's the kitchen. You've got to see the refrigerator! Only two ice-cube trays, and each of them pygmy size."

In spite of such French appurtenances, the whole place had an American air. It was furnished with Scandinavian pieces that looked sterile and modern in comparison to the Louis Quinze style of the suite at the Royal Monceau. But Mindy dutifully complimented Caroline on the decor, and said, "I think it would be simply marvelous to live here the way you do."

"It's fun at first, but actually there's not too much to do."

"Not much to do?" Mindy couldn't believe her ears. "You're joking."

Caroline shook her head, so that her long blond hair brushed her shoulders. "It's not like at home, where there are parties and you get to meet people. The French girls are kept under wraps until they're eighteen, and then they're suddenly grown up. And the boys— well, there just aren't any boys, to speak of."

"You mean French boys? Where are they?"

"At school or home with their mamas, who think American girls are poison."

"Oh, come now!"

"It's true," Caroline insisted. "In Paris good children still marry into the proper families, which means one your parents know."

Mindy was dubious, but she wasn't in a position to argue. "What about American boys who are studying at the Sorbonne, like Dana?" she asked instead.

"Well," said Caroline thoughtfully, "he's pretty shaggy, but he has one advantage over some of the others. He can speak French."

Mrs. Paige came up with a late arrival to be introduced to Mindy, and Caroline at once sauntered over toward Dana, who greeted her cheerfully. Within minutes they were deep in conversation while Mindy began to fume. Why had she ever made such a stupid remark? It was tantamount to handing him over on a silver platter. She found keeping her eyes and her thoughts turned to the person at hand was hard.

Her host reappeared, tucking Mindy's arm through his and drawing her again toward the view from the window. "Today," he told her, "I went out and walked for hours. That's what I do most Sundays, because I like to watch the people—the men in white aprons opening oysters at the corner restaurants, the children and fishermen along the river, the families strolling around in the parks. They have wonderful faces, the French, shrewd and hard-bitten some of them, but full of individuality."

Mindy nodded. She appreciated Mr. Paige's enthusiasm, but her glance kept wandering back to Caroline and Dana, who were laughing over something, leaning together and laughing like old friends. Suddenly Mindy hated Caroline, hated her calculating brown eyes and her yellow hair and her grinning mouth. Getting herself set up for the winter, that's what she's doing, Mindy thought viciously. Can't Dana see that she'll only use him, go out with him merely in order to meet someone else? A girl like her doesn't give two pins for a boy who looks like—like Dylan Thomas!

Aperitif glasses were collected, and a buffet supper was served. It was a simple American meal that was tasty but far from exciting. The food didn't matter anyhow, because Mindy found she wasn't hungry. Every swallow was an effort, as she devised ways to destroy Caroline's influence over Dana once and for all.

Each plot was more fanciful than the last, and all of them impossible. Mindy had to stand by while Caroline gaily made a date with Dana for the following afternoon. "Meet me at school, and I'll take you to a marvelous little bookshop where they give absolutely fantastic student discounts."

Dana agreed with alacrity, while Mindy smiled, murmured pleasant good nights, and asked herself, bitterly, How clever can you get?

Fifteen

"She's something of a charmer, young Caroline. Making quite a play for Dana, wasn't she?" said Alix casually, as she and Mindy were undressing for bed.

Mindy assented with something between a grunt and a snort, then tried to conceal her disaffection by saying, "She was telling me she doesn't know many boys."

"She will," predicted Alix blithely. "When she bats those big brown eyes, the boys forget there isn't a great deal behind them. Girls like Caroline seem to have a recipe for instant success."

Mindy glanced at her cousin surreptitiously. Was she being baited? But Alix, seated at the dressing table creaming her face, looked completely innocent.

Suddenly Mindy felt alone—alone in Paris, alone in the world, defenseless and forlorn. She got into bed quickly, pulled the covers up around her chin, and turned to the wall, yawning conspicuously, then murmuring a perfunctory good night. She closed her eyes, but not to sleep—to think. What had possessed her, to be so stupid as to make that remark about boys at the Sorbonne? Yet why should she care if Caroline chose to make a date with Dana? Actually, it didn't make the slightest difference, one way or another. Dana certainly wasn't handsome and sought after, like Peter Knox.

It occurred to Mindy that tonight was the first time in weeks she had given Peter a passing thought. She wondered idly what he was doing, but not to the point of really caring. He was on the other side of the ocean, and she was no longer involved.

Nor was she involved with Dana. He wasn't in the least romantic, with his spectacles and his rumpled clothes and his passion for books and learning. He had nice eyes, of course, gentle and intelligent, but he certainly was nobody's dream lad. Let Caroline have him, if she liked.

So suppose Dana did meet Caroline after school and they went to this bookstore together. In half an hour Caroline would be bored stiff while Dana prowled among the books. Mindy could see her, pretending an interest that quickly palled, then standing around waiting and becoming increasingly restless. Dana wouldn't even notice. Not Dana! He'd be so absorbed that he wouldn't remember he was with a girl.

Oh, wouldn't he! With a girly type like Caroline a boy would have to be deaf, dumb, and blind not to remember. There was no use trying to console herself with such a ploy.

Console herself? That idea was the silliest yet. Dana was only a casual acquaintance, a friend of her brother and a neighbor of her cousin. Mindy's own life had merely brushed his in passing. Soon she'd be flying home, and he'd be starting classes at the university. Chances were they would never see one another again.

Because they hadn't a thing in common, actually.

Mindy paused. Well, that last bit wasn't quite true. She and Dana had a lot more in common than Dana and Caroline. For one thing, they were both eager and excited about things. Neither one of them would sit around a wonderful city like Paris complaining that there was nothing to do. Caroline was superficial, superficial and much too interested in boys.

For a brief second this conclusion gave Mindy a nice sense of superiority, but then a catch in her throat made her burrow deeper under the bedclothes. Who was she to condemn a person for superficiality when she didn't even have a reason to be jealous of Caroline Paige?

Not a reason in the world! But then if she wasn't jealous why did she feel so wretched? Why, when she finally fell asleep, did she toss and dream? Why, when she awoke the next morning, did the room seem a trifle shabby? Where had the shine gone?

Mindy had no answer. She breakfasted and dressed

and helped Alix ready the salon just as usual. She assisted customers and made out sales slips and listened to people's problems, but one important quality was missing. She didn't take these problems to heart.

Even Alix noticed that her young cousin was listless. "Aren't you feeling well, Mindy?" she asked.

Mindy started, because she had been looking at the clock and thinking that about now Dana would be waiting for Caroline near the *lycée* gate. "I'm all right. I just didn't sleep very well."

"We'll close up shop as early as possible," Alix promised. "Then you can get a nap." She spoke kindly, but she seemed almost as preoccupied as Mindy. "We should be hearing from The Country Cousin," she said after a while. "Paula promised to keep in touch, and we haven't had a letter, but I suppose all our mail will come at once. The French postal service is almost as erratic as their telephones."

Perhaps the French telephone was to blame for the fact that no calls came from Dana either that evening or on Tuesday or Wednesday. Or perhaps he was busy registering for courses. Or conceivably he was occupied with Caroline Paige.

Think about something else, Mindy cautioned herself. Dwelling on anything so trivial is absurd. She went out of her way to be lively and talkative with Alix, and when they walked about Paris together in the long twilight hours she commented appreciatively on glimpses of courtyards through great iron gates, on the cages of singing birds hung against the walls, and on the fragrance of cooking odors drifting up from basement kitchens.

Still, the shine was gone. Paris, although beautiful as ever, seemed a little sad. It was such an old and worn city. Worn cobblestones, worn building façades, worn faces with the gaiety drained away by the passing years.

"Are you homesick, Mindy?" Alix asked.

"No. No, I'm not homesick," Mindy answered truthfully, but the question made her realize that she'd like to be back in her bedroom at the farm, curled up in the four-poster and shut away from the stress of coping with personalities.

"Where would you like to eat? What shall we have for dinner?"

The choice didn't matter. Everything tasted the same.

"We'll have three long lovely days after we ship the collection home," Alix planned encouragingly. "Maybe we can drive to Chartres. You really should see the cathedral. We'll ask Dana to come with us, if you like."

"No." Mindy spoke before she thought and saw the sudden spark of understanding in Alix's eyes. "I mean, his classes will probably have started by then."

"Of course."

Sympathy was even harder to bear than lack of

awareness. By unspoken mutual agreement, the subject of Dana was avoided. Mindy choked down a portion of chocolate mousse and pushed back her chair before Alix had finished her melon. "Maybe we'll have some mail at the hotel," she suggested in place of an excuse.

Her spurious optimism was rewarded. When Alix opened the apartment door, several letters with American postmarks were strewn over the carpet. She bent and scooped them up eagerly. "One for you, Mindy. From your mother. Two from The Country Cousin, and one from New York. Oh, I am anxious to find out how the girls are getting along!"

While Mindy tugged at the flap of the envelope handed her, Alix kicked off her pumps and curled up on the sofa, reading snatches of each communication in turn. "Everything's fine!" she said. "Paula writes, 'Business is booming. Everybody loves our fall clothes and the wool jerseys are selling like crazy. We've reordered several numbers already.' Isn't that great?"

"Marvelous," said Mindy, as she unfolded her mother's letter, but the lilt of enthusiasm was lacking.

Alix glanced at her, frowned, and reported more news. "Irene's mother is worse, poor darling. They're trying some new kind of injections. Arthritis is a devastating disease."

Mindy nodded, her attention captured by the familiar writing. Her mother had nothing special to say.

All was well at the farm, there was a bumper crop of squash in the kitchen garden because of the dry hot summer, and they missed her. Had she made up her mind what she would do this winter? "We'd like nothing better than to have you live at home and go to secretarial school in Reading. Think it over, dear."

Alix opened a second letter, from Jane Scott. " 'All the girls are buying school clothes,' " she quoted. " 'They love the new winter Lillys and those mad plaid slacks.' Good," she said, glancing up from her reading. "I was afraid they might be a little too wild." She turned the page and continued, " 'A stray tiger cat wandered in from the back a couple of days ago, and my sister made the mistake of feeding it. Now it seems to be ours. There's no other earth-shattering news, except that there's been an unexpected flurry of fall engagements, and rumor has it that Peter Knox and Lynn Carstairs are going steady and are apt to send out the glad tidings anytime.' "

Breaking off, Alix sighed. "He's always wanted a rich girl, so maybe Lynn will be the answer."

Mindy nodded. "Maybe." She felt nothing, absolutely nothing, about Peter now. That disastrous dinner date was all but forgotten, and she no longer had the slightest twinge of embarrassment that she had failed to measure up. "He's a curious boy," she said reminiscently. "He seems to have a certain ambition, but it's the wrong kind. If he managed to channel it differently, he might become quite a person. As it is, he doesn't seem real."

Alix nodded. "As Jane would say, he's too good-looking to be true."

Mindy didn't pursue the subject. Her mind had drifted away from her mother's letter to Dana's silence. What had become of his plans for taking her to see the stained glass windows in Sainte Chapelle and for a ride in a *bateau mouche?* "Next week," he had said. Well, *this* was next week, and Wednesday night at that.

She looked at the phone, that irritating French telephone. Either it jingled frantically or became stubbornly silent. Alix was opening her last letter, a typed sheet from which fluttered a slip of paper that looked like a check.

"This is from Harvey Weintraub. He hopes we're taking orders for lots of his clothes and says he can guarantee delivery on everything but number 310. Oh, and listen to this!

" 'We're doing Melinda's little dress in grenadine, lemon, and seaweed for the spring line, and we'll see how well it checks out. She's a talented youngster, and you can tell her from me that after she gets out of Parsons or wherever she's going, there will be a job here waiting for her.' Mindy, isn't that exciting?"

Exciting? The offer was more than exciting. It was so completely unexpected that Mindy could scarcely believe her ears. Suddenly, within the wink of an eye, her future was decided. Why had she ever hesitated? Had she needed just this prod, this first taste of success to make her sure?

"Here, darling. This is for you." Alix was holding out the check, and Mindy walked over for it in a daze. That Mr. Weintraub was buying the design and had paid her generously for it was lovely, but at this particular moment the extra money wasn't important. The important thing was that she knew at last where she was going, and it wasn't to a liberal-arts college or to a Reading secretarial school!

"I wonder if I can still get in," she said aloud.

"Get in where?"

"To Parsons, of course." That Alix should have to ask seemed astonishing.

"You could try," Alix suggested. "You could write at once, tonight. And if it's too late for the fall term you can stay on at The Country Cousin until they find a place for you. It's a marvelous school, if you're sure what you want to do."

"I'm sure," Mindy said softly but definitely. She went to the desk and took a sheet of hotel notepaper from the drawer. "Do you know the address, Alix, or shall I send my application in care of Mr. Weintraub when I thank him for the check?"

Sixteen

The aging concierge looked at the American girl with obvious admiration. She was slim and well-groomed and she had good legs, but it was late at night for her to appear alone in the lobby. Where was Mrs. Moore, that mildly insane shopkeeper with whom she usually came and went?

"May I have an airmail stamp, please, for the United States?"

The concierge searched in his stamp drawer and emerged not with one stamp but with several, which together would serve the purpose, he assured Mindy.

"*Merci beaucoup*," said Mindy politely, and found the change to pay him. "Will this go off right away?" she asked. "*Toute de suite?*"

"*Mais oui, mademoiselle!*" the bald-headed Frenchman assured her, with as much confidence as though he were flying the letter to New York City himself.

Mindy thanked him again, turned away, then came back hesitantly. "Have there been any telephone calls for me, by any chance?"

"You are Miss—Miss . . . ?"

"Hubbard," supplied Mindy. "Melinda Hubbard. Suite 405."

"I think not. Let me see." The concierge began to paw through cubbyholes, above some of which hung room keys. "*Non,*" he said, breaking into French again. "*Non, je regrette—*" Then suddenly he clapped a hand to his forehead, hitting it with such a smack that Mindy started. He returned to the counter with a sheaf of folded white slips. "The day man," he told her apologetically, "has mistaken 504 for 405. He has been ringing the wrong room and putting the messages in the wrong box."

Mindy favored him with such a bright smile that he positively reeled. "It isn't important," she told him dishonestly, then corrected herself. "At least, it isn't important now."

One, two, three, four, five times Dana had phoned and left messages of increasing urgency, the last of which was positively peremptory. "This is my number. Be patient and keep trying. Eventually you'll get through."

Mindy laughed out loud as the self-service elevator ascended to the fourth floor with herself as the single passenger. The long carpeted hall was dimly lit and empty. Succumbing to a sudden impulse she tore the slips into pieces no larger than snowflakes, tossed them up in the air, then skipped merrily along the Aubusson-patterned runner toward the door of the suite. Not at midnight, she was telling herself in a whisper that was almost a song. Never at midnight. Tomorrow morning will be time enough.

In the morning the phone was ringing before Mindy had taken a bite of her buttery *croissant*. Alix, break-fasting propped up in bed, made no effort to answer it, so Mindy leaped for the instrument.

"Hello," she practically purred.

"Mindy!" Dana sounded both relieved and chagrined. "Where have you been?"

"Right here. The day man has been ringing the wrong room."

"Why didn't you call me back?"

"I didn't get your messages until almost twelve o'clock last night, and I thought you'd be asleep by then."

"Well, I wasn't," grumbled Dana. "I was waiting for you to phone, the way I told—asked you to."

"Oh, I *am* sorry." Mindy's voice was as sweet as whipped cream, but she winked slyly at Alix.

"What are you doing tonight?"

"Alix, what are we doing tonight?"

"I said you, not Mrs. Moore," came over the wire in an undertone.

"I can tell you what *I'm* doing tonight," replied Alix. "I'm going to have soup and a salad sent up, and I'm going to bed and read. I need a night off, but then I'm twice your age."

Mindy grinned. "What did you have in mind?" she asked Dana impishly.

"A cheap dinner and a French movie," he said at once.

"That'll be fine," agreed Mindy. "What time?"

They settled on an hour and dined well but inexpensively at the Restaurant des Chauffeurs on the avenue Wagram, then walked over to the Champs Élysées to a cinema. Mindy dozed through half the picture, but she thanked Dana sincerely for a wonderful evening, and with great self-control kept from asking him how he'd enjoyed his excursion with Caroline Paige. Also, because of her innate shyness, she mentioned neither Mr. Weintraub's letter nor her own career plans.

Furthermore, Mindy intuitively knew that tonight wasn't a time for fireworks. It was a night for marking time and for making sure that her friendship with Dana —this friendship she had undervalued until it was threatened—got back on a firm footing.

"When can I see you again?" Dana asked at the hotel door.

"Oh, Dana, I don't know!" Mindy's eyes became troubled. "Tomorrow evening we're going to the Picards, they're French friends of my cousin's. And Saturday we've been given tickets to the opera, which Alix says is important for my education. On Sunday we have to pack the collection, with everything in exact order, for shipment home. That's a job that will take hours."

"But next week you'll be free?"

"I hope so. We fly home Wednesday morning, you know, so that leaves only Monday and Tuesday." Suddenly the days seemed to be compressing themselves like an accordion.

"Are you trying to put me off?"

"Of course not!" Mindy clutched Dana's arm in real distress. He looked so uncertain and hurt that her heart filled with sudden tenderness. "You know I'm not."

There was no question of her sincerity. Dana patted the hand on his arm comfortingly. "I'll phone you Sunday," he promised. "Sunday morning. Don't you dare leave the hotel until you hear from me."

"I won't." Mindy left him reluctantly. "We'll work out some time somehow."

"You're darn tootin' we will," Dana responded, and the inappropriateness of the childish slang made Mindy smile as she walked quickly through the lobby. He likes me, she thought. He really likes me, or he wouldn't have sounded so indignant.

It was lovely to drift through the following days secure in the knowledge that Dana would phone. The dinner party at the Picards was delightful, and the Paris opera house was like a jewel box. Neither experience would Mindy have missed. But Sunday morning was what she looked forward to with the greatest anticipation. Sunday morning and Dana's call.

Quite naturally, she couldn't admit this change of heart to Alix. It was far too secret and personal a thing as yet. But never before had she shivered at the mere thought of a boy's voice. She carried Dana's image around with her, not seeing his rumpled tweeds in her mind's eye, but the expression in his eyes. She recalled too, with quiet pleasure, the keen intelligence of several comments he had made about Paris. He would be a good teacher someday, a fine teacher, with his knack for making a person visualize and appreciate the pictures he painted in words.

Pictures. There was still the Louvre to visit, and the Eiffel Tower. So much of Paris unexplored, and so little time. But if she had to choose between these sights and an afternoon on the river with Dana, Mindy knew what she would do.

The decision, however, was taken out of her hands. Now that the only chore remaining was to repack the collection, Alix was full of buoyancy and plans. "We'll work like beavers all morning," she proposed, "and lunch on the Eiffel Tower. But first we can ride to the very top and drop pennies down like proper tourists. Afterward we might take a bus to the Tuileries and walk through the gardens to the Louvre."

Mindy couldn't dash such enthusiasm. "Can Dana come along?" she asked politely. "He said he was going to call."

"Of course. You know I like Dana. But I thought you'd had some sort of falling out?"

"Not exactly. Anyway, we're friends again."

Alix smiled. "I'm glad to hear it. Then maybe you'd like to reconsider and invite him to go with us to Chartres tomorrow. But don't make a date for Tuesday afternoon, at least not until after six o'clock. I have a surprise for you."

Mindy's heart fell, but she tried to hide her disappointment. Everything Alix was doing was for her: the ride up the tower, the visit to the Louvre, the excursion to Chartres. How could her cousin be expected to guess that suddenly three were a crowd, when all along they had been so companionable?

There was nothing to do but accept the situation with the best possible grace; so Mindy did. When she talked to Dana on the telephone she tried to sound gay as she proposed that he join them, and he accepted, of course, though a trifle glumly. "I was hoping we might have a little time alone."

"We will," Mindy told him over the crackling telephone wire. "We'll talk about it later. O.K.?" With this promise Dana had to be satisfied. He tagged along cheerfully on each consecutive expedition, but on the drive back from Chartres he took matters into his own hands. "I have to go to an orientation lecture at the university tomorrow morning, but I've got the rest of the day free. Can I borrow Mindy for the afternoon and evening, Mrs. Moore?"

"For the evening," said Alix equably, "but not for the afternoon. "We're going to the Dior showing at three thirty."

"We're what?" Mindy's eyes widened. "Dior?" she gasped.

"I told you I had a surprise for you. Our nice concierge phoned and got us two tickets. Maybe we could get a third, Dana. Would you like to come along?"

"Not on your life!" Dana replied. Then he asked, "How long will it take?"

"We should be through by five-thirty."

"I'll meet you outside on the corner," Dana said at once to Mindy. "Wear something warm. We still have to take that ride on a *bateau mouche*."

All Tuesday morning Mindy and Alix shopped for presents to take home. They went to stores that gave tourist discounts and bought small bottles of good perfume for all the country cousins, gloves for Mindy's father, and a scarf for her mother. Then they hurried back to the suite, carrying a picnic lunch of French bread, paté, and pears, which they munched on hungrily as they prepared to shower and change.

Never had Mindy paid more attention to her *toilette*. Copying the Parisian girls she had met, she made up her eyes meticulously and chose her most subtle lipstick, her newest stockings, and her simplest dress. Since the weather was again unseasonably warm, she didn't need a coat. Nevertheless, at Dana's behest, she carried one over her arm when entering the door of the establishment bearing the famous fashion name.

Inside the door a flight of carpeted steps led up to second-floor salons hung with damask draperies and crystal chandeliers. On small gilt chairs a dozen or more women were already seated, and others continued to flow into the rooms in a steady stream. There were Americans and English, elegant Spanish *señoras* dressed with impeccable taste, and French clients who looked very *soignées*, with beautifully tailored suits, stunning leather handbags, and the inevitable French silk scarves. Occasionally there was a girl of Mindy's generation, accompanying her mother, but as a rule the women were Mrs. Moore's age or older, and they looked comparatively well-to-do.

"The season for buyers is over, and the collection won't be as fresh as it was in July," Alix explained, as they waited.

Nevertheless, Mindy was enraptured by her surroundings and by the line of *vendeuses* waiting on the steps with their pads and pencils, all wearing the plain black dresses that were the uniform of their trade. She glanced surreptitiously at the potential customers, particularly at the older women. A few were made up with such artifice that they looked more like puppets than people, yet they still emanated an indefinable chic.

But when the models appeared, announced in both French and English by the numbers of the styles they wore, Mindy really caught her breath in delight. Such attenuated elegance she had never before seen. Each wore with complete assurance successive costumes that had been fitted to their figures. They walked through the salons very rapidly, turning, drawing off coats, swinging their skirts, carrying their heads like princesses.

Their eyes, shadowed by false eyelashes, were kept deliberately remote from the audience. Their hair styles were so far in advance of the fashion that they frequently looked grotesque. Their legs were long and slim. And the dresses themselves Mindy found remarkable. Sometimes they were too extreme to be wearable, but each presented a line and a viewpoint that was new. These designs were those of an unafraid artist, who was determining the shape of things to come.

As always, street and sports costumes were shown

first, followed by late-day dresses. Then finally the models swept past wearing regal ball gowns, which trailed on the floor.

Mindy and Alix whispered together at intervals. "Oh, I like that! Isn't the color marvelous? Look at the line of that coat. We'll be seeing it on Seventh Avenue next year."

Watching with canny attention, then scribbling notes on their programs when a number really interested them, the potential customers could at this point be picked out from the throng of spectators to which Mindy and her cousin belonged.

"Aren't you ever tempted, Alix, to buy just one marvelous original?"

Alix looked thoughtful. "Not really. Although they're exciting and beautiful, these clothes don't fit in with my life. I think appropriateness is more important than anything else in fashion. A dress can be stunning if the occasion is right, but if the occasion is wrong—" She broke off and shrugged descriptively.

Mindy, however, still had stars in her eyes when applause for the pearl-encrusted wedding gown that climaxed the showing died away. Through the crush on the stairs she went downward in a daze, and not until she emerged into the daylight and saw Dana hovering near the corner did she return to comparative reality.

Alix said quick good-byes. "I'm joining a friend for

dinner," she told Dana belatedly. "Don't wait up, Mindy. I may be late."

"We may be late too," retorted Dana blithely. "After all, it's our last night."

"Don't say that. Don't even think it," Mindy begged, as her cousin walked away. "Let's pretend we'll always be in Paris, that nothing will ever change."

Dana laughed. "You wouldn't like that, Mindy. Change is the very essence of living. It makes us grow."

"No philosophizing," Mindy commanded. "Let's eat, drink, and be merry, for tomorrow I fly."

Dana groaned. "Ouch. That one hurt."

"What can you expect? I'm not bright like you."

"No, you're bright like yourself." Playfully, Dana pulled Mindy's arm through his and turned her in the direction of the river. "It's not too far. Let's walk."

The air was soft, and it seemed more like spring than September. The sidewalk cafés were filling with people, and the flower sellers were busy. Taxis were scurrying hither and yon, and near the river a balloon vendor was still offering his tempting, bright-colored wares to every passing child.

While Dana stood in a ticket line for the *bateau mouche* Mindy bought postcards, so absorbed in the process of selection that she didn't hear him approach.

"Hey, aren't you a little late? You'll get home ahead of the cards."

"Oh, these aren't to send. They're to keep," Mindy explained, and clutched them to her almost defensively. "This winter I can look at them and remember how marvelous it's all been."

"And think of me?" Dana's voice was half-serious, half-teasing.

"And think of you," replied Mindy soberly. "Without you Paris wouldn't have been—"

"Don't start talking in the past tense yet!" Dana cautioned when she hesitated. "Come on. They're letting people aboard."

Finding seats on deck near the front of the boat, Dana settled Mindy close to the rail and insisted that she put her coat around her shoulders. "It can be chilly on the river when we get under way."

Mindy was acquiescent, because she rather enjoyed such solicitude. She felt warm and alive and filled with a bubbling joy to be in this special place at this special time. While she obediently admired the bridges under which they moved, the public buildings they passed, and the impressive buttresses of Notre Dame when seen from the rear, none of the sights was as important as the nearness of Dana, the touch of his jacket sleeve on her arm, the warmth with which he suddenly squeezed her hand as they approached the Pont Neuf.

"There!" he cried. "That's one of the views I love."

Ahead of them a middle-aged couple were laboriously getting acquainted. The woman, in a pink tweed suit, looked like an American school teacher, and her companion, a dapper Frenchman who spoke passable English, apparently had met her only recently. In clearly audible tones they were probing each other's past. Apparently the man was a widower and the rather personable woman a maiden lady on her first trip abroad. Flattered by the Frenchman's attentions, she was being charming yet cautious. Amused, then touched by this little vignette, Mindy called Dana's attention to the pair in a whisper.

"Would you say she was 'bridaling'?"

Dana chuckled. "Very definitely."

"Don't they seem awfully old for that sort of thing?"

"On the contrary. You seem awfully young."

"I'm not. I'll be eighteen before you get back next spring. And maybe I'll be living in New York," Mindy bragged. Then suddenly the couple ahead was forgotten, and she found herself pouring out to Dana all the plans burgeoning for her future. "It's the most wonderful feeling," she told him, her eyes alight with enthusiasm, "to know precisely what I want to do!"

Dana nodded understandingly. "But aren't you getting into an overcrowded field?"

"No field is overcrowded if you're good enough," Mindy replied firmly.

"And you plan to be good enough."

"I do."

"Oh, Mindy, Mindy, you're marvelous!" Dana said softly. "Where's the girl I took to Robin Hood Dell? Whatever happened to Jack's little sister? Presto-change-o, and you're a young woman, right before my very eyes!"

"You mustn't tease me," Mindy begged. "This is serious."

"I know it is." Dana spoke tenderly. "And I love you for it. But Mindy, while you're growing so fast, don't grow too far away from me."

"I couldn't," Mindy promised. "Can't you tell, Dana, that I'm growing toward you all the time?"

The boat had rounded the Ile de la Cité and was starting on the return trip. The Paris sky was streaked with pink and purple and a wind had risen. Dana slid his arm along the back of the seat and pulled Mindy closer. "I'm cold, even if you aren't," he said, "and spring seems much too far away."

Betty Cavanna grew up in Haddonfield, New Jersey, and was graduated from Douglass College, where she majored in journalism. It was during her work for Westminster Press in Philadelphia that she became interested in writing stories herself, and in 1943 she became a full-time writer of books for young people. She holds an honorary membership in Phi Beta Kappa for her outstanding contribution to the field of juvenile literature.

Although the characters in *The Country Cousin* are fictional, the background is completely authentic. The author worked briefly selling clothes in shops and discovering what goes on behind the scenes where packages are unwrapped and merchandise is ticketed. She went on buying trips to the New York wholesale market and to Paris on an expedition like that described in the final chapter of the book. Helping out with all this research was Dorothy Lewis Lummis, the owner of the real dress store, The Country Cousin.

In private life Miss Cavanna is Mrs. George Russell Harrison. She and her husband live in Concord, Massachusetts.